About the Author

Magenta is the pen name of a dreamer. One who enjoys all the smutty deliciousness romance can bring. One who knows how much real life can bring you down and knows the value of being able to escape into a pretend world. Pretend worlds, where there is always a happy ever after.

I0593381

Also by Magenta

Dreamy Delights

ARBOR VITAE COVEN
BOOK TWO

MAJENTA

NEIGHPALM PUBLISHING

For my mum, Jill. I wouldn't be who I am without your love, guidance, and support.
Thank you

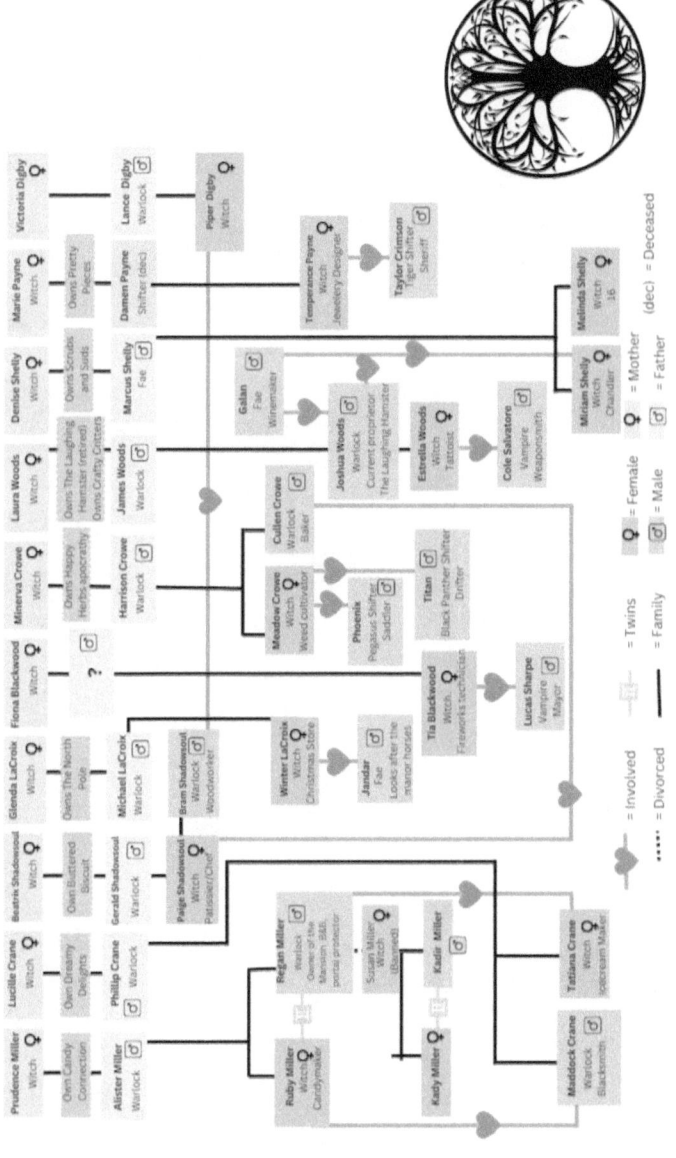

Victoria Digby ♀

Lance Digby ♂ Warlock

Piper Digby ♀ Witch

Marie Payne ♀ Witch · Owns Pretty Pieces

Damen Payne ♂ Shifter (dec)

Temperance Payne ♀ Witch · Jewellery Designer

Taylor Crimson ♂ Tiger Shifter · Sheriff

Denise Shelly ♀ Owns Candelabras and Spells

Marcus Shelly ♂ Fae

Melinda Shelly ♀ Witch · 16

Miriam Shelly ♀ Witch · Chandler

Laura Woods ♀ Witch · Owns The Laughing Hamster (retired)

James Woods ♂ Warlock · Owns Crafty Critters

Galan ♂ Fae · Wiremaster

Joshua Woods ♂ Warlock · Current proprietor The Laughing Hamster

Estrella Woods ♀ Witch · Tattooist

Cole Salvatore ♂ Vampire · Weaponsmith

Minerva Crowe ♀ Witch · Owns Happy Herbapoocary

Harrison Crowe ♂ Warlock

Cullen Crowe ♂ Warlock · Baker

Meadow Crowe ♀ Witch · Weed cultivator

Phoenix ♂ Pegasus Shifter · Saddler

Titan ♂ Black Panther Shifter · Drifter

Fiona Blackwood ♀ Witch

? ♂

Tia Blackwood ♀ Witch · Fireworks Technician

Lucas Sharpe ♂ Vampire · Mayor

Glenda LaCroix ♀ Witch · Owns The North Pole

Michael LaCroix ♂ Warlock

Evan Shadowood ♂ Warlock · Woodworker

Winter LaCroix ♀ Witch · Christmas Store

Jandar ♂ Fae · Looks after the interior horses

Beatrix Shadowood ♀ · Owns Buttered Biscuit

Gerald Shadowood ♂ Warlock

Paige Shadowood ♀ Witch · Potioner/Chef

Lucille Crane ♀ Witch · Owns Dreamy Delights

Phillip Crane ♂ Warlock

Regan Miller ♂ Warlock · Owner of the Medium SAE portal generator

Susan Miller ♀ Witch · (Retired)

Kadir Miller ♂

Prudence Miller ♀ Witch · Owns Candy Confection

Alister Miller ♂ Warlock

Ruby Miller ♀ Witch · Candymaker

Kady Miller ♀

Tatiana Crane ♀ Witch · Icecream Maker

Maddock Crane ♂ Warlock · Blacksmith

♀ = Female ♂ = Male

(dec) = Deceased

♀ = Mother ♂ = Father

💗 = Involved

⬡⬡ = Twins

___ = Family

••••• = Divorced

Fae Realm

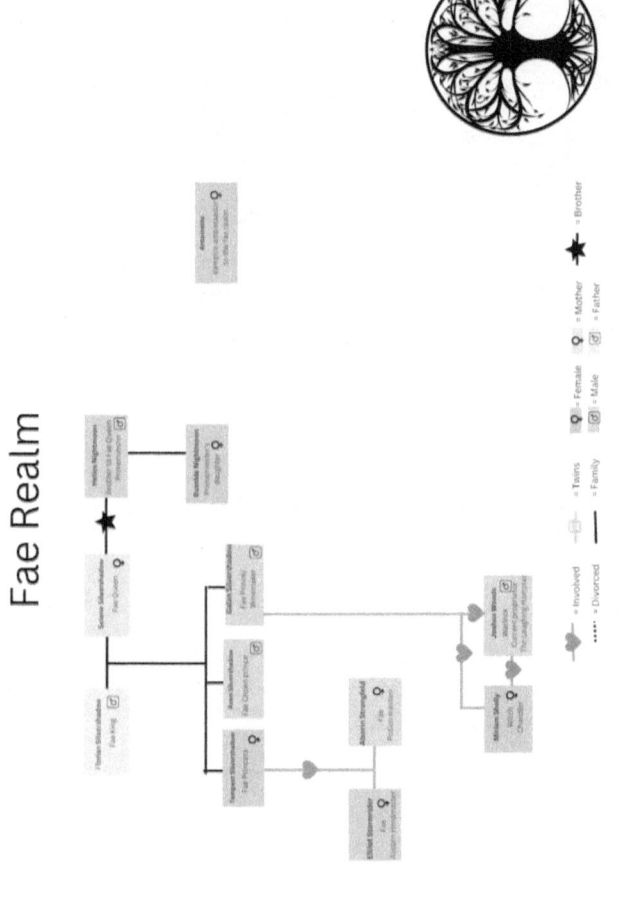

Vampire Realm

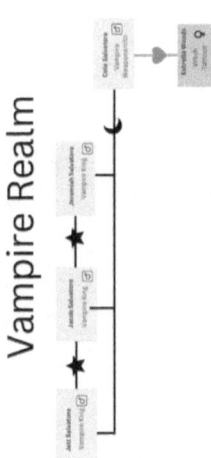

- = Involved
- = Divorced
- = Twins
- = Family
- = Female
- = Male
- = Mother
- = Father
- = Brother
- = Cousin

Prologue

"This meeting of the Matrons of Morbank Island may come to order," Prudence Miller announces as she bangs her gavel on the lectern in front of her. The excited chatter of the ladies around her dulls more quickly than usual, but they have so many things to discuss and not much time.

"As I'm sure you all know by now, the spell worked," she announces, but she shakes her head somewhat ruefully. "Sort of! My Ruby has returned."

The ladies surrounding her burst into applause, some a little less enthusiastically than others, but that's to be expected. Pru sweeps a sympathetic look around the room.

"I know it's not the outcome we expected, but it's a start. There are some very dark forces working against us, but never fear, ladies, we will overcome these obstacles, and I have no doubt that we will prevail."

This time the round of applause is more enthusiastic.

"As we meet, Ruby is on a plane to Italy to drag Tatiana home. We think it's possible some of them are just too far away to be affected by the spell, so she is armed with the same anti-negativity potion that we used on Maddock."

Looking around the room, she casts a spell to ensure privacy. "We have anchored Tatiana's potion to Regan. I know," she says, holding her hands up. "I can see your skeptical looks. Ruby and I decided if we anchored the potion to someone in the town who is unaffected that we would have a better chance of overcoming it. It's just a light anchor, and no one's forcing anyone together or anything. I changed the spell so that it doesn't need to be sealed with a kiss. It will fade eventually, and hopefully, by that time, we will have defeated whoever is responsible. If they do kiss and seal it permanently, however, I know that I, for one, wouldn't mind more grandbabies, and Lucille and Phillip feel the same way," she explains, her lips stretching into a cheeky smile.

Lucille nods her head enthusiastically. "I am praying to the goddess that Ruby is successful. I'm so grateful that Maddock is sorted out and we got rid of Sheree. I love having Melly work for me, but I'm ready to retire. I want to start enjoying life a little more. I'd rather ask for forgiveness than permission," she states stubbornly, crossing her arms.

"One by one we'll drag those girls home, kicking and screaming if need be, but I'm sure it won't come to that. I'm also thinking we'll need to perform the same spell we did before on the full moon, adding in each returned girl's power. By the next full moon, hopefully both Ruby and Tatiana will be able to add their power to it."

Everyone shows their agreement with head nods, murmuring, "Yes."

"So that is the daughter situation update. Now, on to another pressing problem—the portal. Over the last few weeks, we have had a few issues. The portal has faded briefly three times. Luckily no one was attempting to realm travel when this happened, but we've had to limit travel to twice a week until we can get it fixed. Tuesdays and Fridays will be travel times. In short, we need an influx of tourists. Regan has scheduled more meetings with the heads of the fae, vampire, and shifter realms to finalize his realm tour programs. They have been approved, so now it is just a matter of working out the nitty- gritty details."

"I don't understand this at all," Fiona Blackwood says, shaking her head. "We have had periods of low tourism before. Let's face it, a hundred years ago we didn't have any tourists at all, and the portal still functioned perfectly. There must be something else that is interfering with the portal's power."

"What about on the realm side of the portal?" Minerva Crowe asks. "Maybe we need to send someone in to investigate that side."

Pru purses her lips before nodding her head. "Yes, but we need to be diplomatic about it. We can't accuse anyone or point fingers, or they will get upset."

"What about asking Regan to keep an eye out for things when he goes for his final meetings?" Beatrix adds.

"What about the mayor? He's a vampire, so maybe he can put some feelers out?" Denise Shelly suggests. "He's so kind, I'm sure he would help if we explain the situation."

Prudence's heart sinks. She was hoping to keep it a secret for now, but the coven does have a responsibility to the town and the other supernaturals living in it.

"You're all right. It's time to share this and get some more heads and hearts working on the problem. I wouldn't want the paranormal council to accuse us of not doing everything we can."

"So we decided to come to you for help. It's become a whole town issue now, not just the coven's. Someone is out to destroy us. The Miller's candy store was vandalized a few weeks ago, as well as Ruby's car. Things are starting to escalate," Pru says, updating Mayor Lucas Sharpe on the issues surrounding the island, the coven, and the portal.

Sitting behind a wide, wooden desk, Mayor

Sharpe wears a stylish gray suit that makes his eyes look even grayer than usual.

The frown on his face grew increasingly more pronounced as the story progressed. Blowing out a deep breath as she finishes, he sits back in his chair with an expression of exasperation crossing his features as he processes the information. "You should have come to me sooner, Pru. I know I haven't been mayor of this town for very long, and that I'm still a stranger compared to the founding families of the island, but I care, and I want to be able to help the community any way I can."

She wiggles under his stern gaze but straightens her back and replies, "Yes, I know, but we all make mistakes. Trust is a little thin on the ground at the moment, but I will endeavor to do better," she promises, looking a little embarrassed.

"Well, pointing the finger of blame is not going to help the situation now, Mayor Sharpe. At least Mom realized her error and has now fixed it. Let's move on, shall we?" Regan suggests, breaking the tension in the room.

The mayor nods. "Yes, of course, and what's this Mayor Sharpe crap, Regan? We've known each other too long for such formalities. It sounds like you already have some plans in the works. I'll put out some feelers of my own, but let's work on a few more things to bring the tourists back."

Both Pru and Regan nod their heads.

Regan speaks up. "Well, I have my realm tourism

plans in the works, and if I get my approvals, we should be ready to start by Halloween. I thought maybe the manor could run a haunted house for Halloween this year and sell tickets. Also, with coven help, we could turn the open grassy space into a cornfield and run a maze as well. We could have hayrides through the orchards and apple picking, and maybe an apple cider stand and pumpkin carving. We could even bring in a band and make it a real town event. It could double as the launch for the tours too."

The look on Pru's face changes from worried to enthusiastic. "Regan, that's a fantastic idea. What do you think, Mayor?"

He has a thoughtful expression on his face. "That's a great start. How about the coven starts working on that, Pru? Regan, you concentrate on the tours, because I think that will be very popular. I have an idea about the band, so leave that to me."

Pru and Regan nod.

"Also, let's keep the momentum going. I was thinking we can have a Thanksgiving celebration in the town square. Maybe a feast?"

Pru is practically bouncing on her chair in excitement. "Oh, and some fireworks! We can call it Feast and Fireworks, and sell turkey legs and pie and maybe have some old-fashioned games and dress up in period pieces. What a great idea!"

"Okay, so we have some ideas. Let's keep in contact, schedule a few meetings, and get this town revitalized. Once we get the portal issue fixed, we can deal with whoever is behind the spells." A grave look crosses the mayor's face. "When I find out who has messed with my town, they will be sorry."

Pru shudders at the violence in his tone. Up until now, one could forget that the mayor is a vampire, but after the cold, callous way he just said that, she wouldn't want to be in the shoes of the person responsible.

"Also, I have another issue. It's not just supernaturals being affected by the spell. Young humans are also leaving the island," Regan tells Lucas. "It's become a huge issue out at the manor. With the older locals retiring and the young ones leaving, I'm essentially down to only a few employees, and that does not go over well with guests. I need to employ some new people—quite a few, actually."

"Okay, but what does that have to do with me?" A look of confusion crosses Lucas's face.

"Because the island has the portal, the population has been strictly controlled in the past and approval needs to be given to move here, so I need your permission and consent to advertise and interview new employees," Regan tells him.

His confused expression clears, and Lucas sits back in his chair, relaxing. "Sure, man, as long as they have no records and you run background checks on them all, that's fine. Are you employing humans or supes?"

"I'm thinking of sticking to supes. Humans are a little jumpy at times, even the ones who were raised on the island." Smiles cross both Pru's and Lucas's faces when Regan says this. "I mean, I won't dismiss hiring a human, but I will advertise through supe social media first and see how it goes."

Lucas stands up, and Pru and Regan follow suit. "Alright, it looks like we have some work to do. Shall we reconvene in a fortnight and discuss what plans we have made?"

Both Pru and Regan agree, and after shaking hands, they leave the mayor's office a little lighter than they were when they first arrived.

CHAPTER
One

Tatiana

Ruby's cheerful voice chattering in my ear about all the changes she made to the candy store is a perfect distraction from my dark, dreary thoughts as the ferry pulls into Morbank Island. I watch as it docks against the jetty and big ropes are thrown to the waiting dock worker. The engines power down, and the noise of the ferry fades, leaving behind the sound of the water lapping against the pylons.

As I look out across the river, I watch the early morning mist drift slowly along the banks, the overcast sky lending a bleak reflection to the smooth surface. The morning perfectly matches my mood.

I wasted eighteen months on that bastard. I thought we had something good. Before I left, Marco tried to tell me that it was a one-time thing, that he had never done it before, that he loved me and wanted to marry me. Maybe Ruby is right and it was backlash from the spell, a way of guaranteeing I return home. Either way, I wasn't hanging around to listen to his lies and false promises.

Letting out a big sigh, I sit up straighter as she drives her old Mustang off the ferry and heads down Main Street. The leaves on the trees have started to change colors and vacate the branches. Small piles gather under each one, ready for collection. The trees look bare and lonely in the gloomy weather. Fall is on its way, and Halloween is just around the corner. The prelude to winter is not the most ideal time to revitalize an ice-cream store, but I'm going to give it my best go.

We pull into a parking lot not far from Dreamy Delights, and Ruby turns off the engine. Looking everywhere else other than the entrance, I notice the Halloween decorations in the store window of Candy Connection—cauldrons full of fall-colored candy, a witch flying on her broomstick suspended above black cats, and skeletons. All are delightfully witchy and kitschy. A new awning suspended above the door and a fresh coat of paint on the window frame draws the eye and catches your attention.

Looking at the store next door, I feel a stab of guilt. There are no signs of festive decorations, and a tired, faded awning greets my gaze. Mom was always one of the first to drag out holiday decorations, and between Halloween and Valentine's Day, there wasn't a day that went by when we didn't have decorations in the window. The lump in my throat grows bigger in shame.

Another big sigh leaves my mouth as I look down the quiet street. Before I left, Main Street would have been bustling with tourists at this time of day. Close to lunch, people would be out sampling the delights of the Buttered Biscuit or having a quiet lunchtime meal at the Laughing Hamster with a pint of beer to go along with the scrumptious food. The stores would be brimming with young and old alike, attracted to the bright and beautiful displays in the windows.

Looking at the storefronts now, I see a few displays, but the eye-catching, attention-grabbing zing is missing. The lights aren't even on in Pretty Pieces, and the display window is dark. Turning back to Dreamy Delights, I close my eyes and lean my head back against the seat.

"What's wrong, Tatiana? Talk to me," Ruby murmurs quietly, putting a hand on my knee.

Looking at her, I can see the worry in her eyes. "What if she doesn't want to see me? What if she won't forgive—" A hand presses against my mouth, stopping me from finishing the sentence.

"No! Just stop that right now. She's your mom, and she missed you, and just like mine forgave me and was thrilled to see me, so will your mom."

Tears well, threatening to overflow. Ruby can see the indecision in my eyes when I look back at her, and a sympathetic smile crosses her face. Starting the car, she backs out of the parking spot and heads away from Dreamy Delights.

"You know what? Let's get a drink. A little bit of liquid courage never hurt anyone." She winks at me. "Josh's partner makes the most exquisite wine. Everything will seem so much better after a glass." She pulls into the Hamster's parking lot and stops the car. We both get out and start toward the tavern, but she grabs my hand, stopping me. "Tatiana, I know it all feels overwhelming right now, but trust me on this, your mom is going to be thrilled to see you. I was afraid to face my parents, too, when I first got back and realized the magnitude of my indifference. I thought they would never forgive me, but they did, and Lucille will forgive you." A frown crosses her face. "In fact, there's nothing to forgive. Someone else is responsible, and we'll find out who it is, and when we do, we'll make them pay." Ruby has this fierce look on her face, and her hands clench into fists.

A burst of laughter explodes from my mouth, and for the first time in days, I feel lighter.

She raises her eyebrows in question. "What the freaking hell are you laughing at?"

Tears stream down my face, and it's hard to talk around the laughter. "Oh my god, Ruby, you should see your face. You were all fierce and shit. Be careful, I might start calling you the wicked witch of Morbank. If the wind changes, your face might be stuck like that, and children will run in fright."

She doesn't say a word, just shoots her middle

finger at me and walks into the Hamster muttering, "See if I try to give you a pep talk ever again, bitch."

Still laughing, I follow after her.

After a couple of glasses of wine and catching up with Josh and his gorgeous partner Galan, Ruby and I find ourselves back in her car.

"Where to now? You want to head to my place and settle in?" she asks, starting the car.

"Yours?" I ask in confusion.

She looks at me and then grins guiltily. "Sorry, I never asked what you wanted to do. I just assumed you would stay with me for a while until you were settled in. Do you want me to drop you at your mom's instead?" she inquires.

Shaking my head, I look in the direction of the ice-cream store. "No, Ruby, it's time to swallow my pride. Take me to Mom."

She drives the short distance to Dreamy Delights, stopping in front. "Would you like me to come with you?" she asks, putting the car into park.

Shaking my head, I climb out. "No, I need to do this on my own, but thanks. Can you pop the trunk?" She smiles encouragingly at me and flicks a switch. Going to the back, I grab my backpack and slam it closed before returning to the front and leaning in. "Thanks so much, Ruby, for everything."

She nods and smiles. "Call me when you can."

Closing the door, I stand and wave as she drives down the street.

I blow out a breath and turn to face the music. Surveying the front of the ice-cream shop, I wonder why we never put outside seating on the tree-lined grass section between the parking area and the stores. A few tables with some umbrellas would be lovely in summer.

Movement in the corner of my eye draws my attention. A bunny is hopping across the space of land between the next store and us, and the wheels in my brain start turning. It's about a hundred feet wide, and grassy with a grove of small trees. The council keeps it mowed, but for as long as I can remember, nothing has ever been done to it. When we were kids, we would run around and play on it, and I'm sure it's still used for that now. An idea is building—something to run past Mom and Dad if they are still talking to me. With that thought, I stop stalling and get on with it.

I walk across the damp grass to the entrance. My heart is in my throat and my blood is rushing through my veins, throbbing in my ears. As I push the glass door open, the familiar sound of the chimes and the smell of waffle cones cooking bring me a sense of peace.

"Won't be a moment," my mom's musical voice calls out from behind the counter, causing my nerves to bounce in anticipation.

Straightening my back and lifting my head, I look

around the store. Nothing has changed. The same red vinyl booths are cracked and faded, and the little menu plaques sitting on each table are cloudy and scratched. Grabbing one, I read the available options, which are still the same as it was when I was a kid. Nothing has changed for many years.

Frowning, I put it back and walk across the scuffed and faded black and white vinyl that is lifting in a few sections. Looking around, I decide that Ruby had the right idea. A complete makeover and menu change is going to be a good start. Throw in a few new options, and I think we'll be on our way to revitalize this little section of Morbank Island.

I step up to the ice-cream freezers and study the selection of flavors. The old standard ice-cream fare is available. There's chocolate, vanilla, strawberry, chocolate mint, and every child's favorite—bubblegum. They provide a rainbow of colors, but they are still the same typical offerings. My excitement starts to poke its head through my nerves. I have ideas and thoughts that I worked on during the plane ride back from Italy—new and exciting things to try—but first, my mom.

"What can I get you?" A bustling figure behind the counter draws my attention. She's drying her hands on a towel and not looking up. Her pale skin is duller than usual, and her curly dark hair is in disarray. My mother was always well put together and stylish. She'd say, "Just because I make ice cream, Tatiana, doesn't mean I can't look good while doing it." She also looks shorter and slighter than I remember. Baggy and ill-fitted, her cardigan has a hole near the pocket. A wave of guilt swamps me, and I steady myself against the counter.

When I realize she hasn't said anything else, my gaze shoots to hers. Her eyes are wide, and her already pale face has lost even more color. "Tatiana? Is that you?"

"Hi, Mama. I'm home," I tell her, looking everywhere but at her. I don't want to see what her next reaction will be—the possible rejection.

A loud sob escapes her mouth, drawing my eyes back to her. With tears streaming down her face, she rushes around the counter before throwing herself at me. Her thin arms wrap around my shoulders, strong despite how they look.

"Oh, my baby! Pru said Ruby had gone to get you, but I didn't want to get my hopes up after all the times I tried to call and speak to you, and you ignored my calls or cut me off every time I tried to get you to come home."

"I know, I'm so sorr—" I start to apologize, but she cuts me off.

"No, Tatiana, I don't want to hear it. There is nothing to apologize for. We won't speak of it again." Pulling away from me, she looks around. "Where's Marco? Is he still outside?"

Sighing, I pull away and sit in one of the booths. She goes to the coffee machine and raises a cup. "Coffee?" she asks, and I nod.

"Yes, please. No, Mom, Marco isn't here."

She turns around, briefly abandoning what she's

doing. "Oh? He isn't? Will he be coming soon?" she asks, her voice hopeful, and then her face falls. "Or will you be going back to Italy?"

"Oh, Mom, no," I reassure her. "No, I won't be returning to Italy."

Her smile is blinding, and the relief on her face is apparent. "So he'll be coming here then?" she questions, curiosity now burning in her eyes.

Blowing out another long breath, I shake my head. "No, Mom, he won't. When Ruby came to get me, and I returned to our apartment to pack, I found him in bed with another woman. He claimed it was a one-time thing, but…" I shrug, my anger rising. "But I don't believe him, and I have no interest in forgiving him."

She brings the cups of coffee over to the booth, sits down opposite me, and reaches out a hand. "Oh, sweetheart. I'm sorry."

I squeeze her hand before grabbing my coffee and blowing over the top. I take a sip, the liquid warming and soothing, and a smile curves my lips. "Ruby thinks it has to do with the spell."

My mum gasps, a hand coming to her mouth. "Consequences! Oh no. I'm sorry." A guilty look crosses her face.

"Don't be, Mom. I'm happy to be home, and I think if a little spell encouraged him to cheat, then maybe it wasn't meant to be. Temptation is always around, and being weak is not an excuse."

The guilty look leaves her face. "Good, I never liked the asshole anyway." My eyebrows rise in shock, and before I can ask why, she continues, "He was rude every time I called. He told me he would pass on the message, but you never called back. I know now that was partly the spell's fault, but there's still a little bit of me that thinks he had something to do with it. But never mind, what's done is done." She takes a sip of coffee.

The chimes above the door ring awkwardly as the door flies open with a bang. It sounds like a small child is in a hurry to get to the ice cream, but it's not a small child behind the door, it's my brother Maddock. He looks around, his eyes wild, until he stops on me. "Tatticake, you're back."

Hmm, looks like Ruby's lips have been flapping. He strides toward me and yanks me out of the booth, wrapping his arms around me. He smells like smoke and metal, and he has dirt smudged across his cheek. My face is smooshed into his broad chest, so his voice rumbles through my ears.

"Thank goodness."

Pulling back from his embrace, I punch him on the shoulder.

"Ow, Tatticake, what was that for?" he whines, and the joy in my heart at seeing my brother overrides my annoyance at his whiny tone.

"Dude, that was for defiling my friend."

He splutters, stammering excuses, but I hold out my hand, and he stops.

I kiss him on the cheek. "I couldn't be happier. It's been a long time coming."

A huge grin crosses his face, and he blushes

slightly. "Thank you." He places a kiss on my fore-head and then slides into the booth next to Mom, giving her a kiss too.

A hand taps my shoulder, drawing my attention, and I turn to find my dad standing behind me with a frown on his face. My stomach drops.

Crap, is he going to make up for the lack of anger in Mom? I didn't even notice him enter, since Maddock had captured my attention. We just stand here staring at each other, our eyes locked in concentration. A small smile tickles my lips as the staring contest continues, but I manage to keep a straight face. This was a thing we would do when I was a teenager, him trying to assess whether I was telling the truth or not. I would always cave, even if I wasn't lying.

My eyes start to well, the strain of not blinking getting to me. His nostrils flare, and it's all over. Laughter escapes from my mouth in a blast as I lose the contest.

"Ah, baby, I've still got it," he says, wrapping his arms around me and pulling me in. He also smells like forge and fire. He must have been working with Maddock today. I know Ruby told me he is basically retired, but he gets bored because Mom has to come to the ice-cream shop, so he likes to go in and help out.

Well, now that I'm home, that's going to change, and they can both enjoy their retirement together.

CHAPTER
Two

Tatiana

Seeing my family and knowing none of them are upset with me is a huge weight lifted off my shoulders. We sit for a couple of hours and catch up while Mom serves the few customers who walk through our doors. The small number surprises me. Even heading into winter, we always had a steady stream of tourists who had a craving for ice cream. Hmm, that has me thinking.

"Mom, do we have an enchantment on the island or this shop that encourages people to spend money?"

Her mouth drops open in shock, and she aggressively replies, "Of course not! We are not crooks or criminals. That would be dishonest."

"Okay, Mom, settle down," I tell her, holding my hands up. "I guess it was just your amazing ice cream keeping them coming back for more." A pleased look crosses her face, the frown lines smoothing out. "I was thinking about making a few changes and spicing things up a bit. How do you feel about that? Similar to what Ruby did over at Candy." I gesture around the shop. "It's time for a makeover, don't you think?" Mom and Dad both nod their heads with murmurs of agreement.

Maddock has a smug look on his face. "I wondered how long it would take for you to start. Did Ruby talk your ears off about the candy store on the way home?"

Nodding, I ask, "What about that open space next door? It's never been used by anyone. Who does it belong to?"

Mom and Dad exchange looks, and Dad shrugs his shoulders. "I'm not sure, honey. It's always been vacant. Maybe we could go over to city hall and find out?"

"Okay, let's do that, because I want to turn it into an outdoor entertainment area more family-friendly than the Hamster. The pub caters to young adults, and you can take your kids there for lunch or dinner, but it gets a bit rowdy. If we can find out who owns it and get permission, then it would be a great spot for families to meet. We could put in a playground and maybe a skate park, and cover half of it for winter or use a spell to keep the weather out. We could have Gerald and Bram build us some outdoor furniture for when summer returns."

Another idea comes to me.

"Or better yet, how about you and Maddock

build a fire pit? We could use another spell so kids can't fall into it. That will keep the area warm and dry and usable during winter. If we put in a basketball court down the back, we could possibly use it as an ice rink in winter. We could even build a bandstand and have outdoor concerts, and give young people and families a place to hang out and get some fresh air during winter." As I take a breath, another idea hits me. "We could serve hot chocolate and some warmer options over winter. Maybe we could convince the Millers to go halves with us, and they can make S'more kits to sell and be used at the pit too. If we use a spell to keep the weather out, we could put couches, bean bags, and things in there and make it a real destination."

My ideas are building on top of each other, and the words just keep flowing from my mouth. Mom, Dad, and Maddock have huge grins on their faces as they listen.

"I also have some ideas for menu changes. Maybe offer a few different things apart from the standard scoops and sundaes. Before I stopped and stayed in Italy, I traveled and visited ice-cream stores all over Europe. The different ways of serving it now are unbelievable. I want to start offering more choices. Also, let's makeover the inside of the shop." I gesture to the graffitied tabletop. "I think it's time. I can still see where Ruby and I carved our initials when we were ten."

Mom looks surprised and goes to say something, but I keep going.

"New booths, new tables, a cozy nest of couches in the back corner, and maybe a bookcase with local authors and some board games. Add a fresh coat of paint and new flooring, and the place will look amazing. Let's offer free Wi-Fi and a place for devices to be plugged into at every table. Encourage studying, and the teenagers will come in droves. Lastly, let's build a fireplace inside so it will cozy things up in here for winter as well, maybe get a jukebox." A whoosh of air escapes as I flip back against the booth, my tirade of ideas finally finished.

Dad sat with his hand against his cheek while he listened to my ramblings, but now he slaps it down on the table, making me jump in surprise. He stands up, rubs his hands together, and looks excited. "All of that sounds like quite a plan. I'll go to the records office now and see if I can find out who owns the land outside. We need to get their permission for any of your outside ideas, so the sooner we find out, the better." He moves out of the booth then bends down to give Mom and me a kiss on the cheek. "Glad to have you back, honey." He waves goodbye and hurries out.

I look at Mom, worried it was all too much, but she wears a grin a mile wide. "Thank goodness Pru worked out what was wrong. I knew there had to be a reason you weren't coming home or even talking to me very often. They are great ideas, Tatiana. How about we get you settled at home and then sit down and have a brainstorm and get all this written down?

We can plan it all out and speak to Gerald and Bram as soon as possible."

Maddock gets up and helps himself to the ice-cream fridge, putting a scoop in a cup before coming back to the table. Mom and I frown at him, and Mom crosses her arms in annoyance. A sheepish expression crosses his face as he shoves a spoonful of his favorite rum and raisin into his mouth. "Sorry, I'm hungry. I didn't think about you two," he mumbles around a mouthful of ice cream.

Mom shakes her head, and I decide to broach a delicate subject.

"Mom, what about changing up the flavors a bit?"

A stubborn look crosses her features. "These are my family's recipes, Tatiana, and you know they haven't changed since we've been selling ice cream."

I arch my eyebrow at her. "Do you think that might be part of the problem? Look, I'm not saying to get rid of the old favorites, we just need to offer more. Try to come up with something we've never done before."

Maddock wears a thoughtful look on his face as he pokes his plastic spoon at me. "Ruby is using some of the sparkling fairy wine Galan makes in one of her fudge recipes. What about something like that?" he suggests. "And don't forget, Mom, you had marijuana written on the whiteboard out back a few weeks ago."

I look at her in surprise, and she appears sheepish. "Well, your suggestion had merit now that it's legal here in Canada. I didn't get very far on that though," she admits.

"What a fabulous idea," I tell her. "We can work on it, and yes, Maddock, that's the sort of thing I'm talking about. I'm not sure the wine will work for ice cream, maybe a sorbet, but it's along the right line of thinking." Excitement builds as an idea forms. "What about using products from the other realms instead of Earth? We can see what kind of produce I can source from there."

Mom sits up straight. "You could go with Regan when he goes to finalize the realm tours. He wouldn't mind, would he, Maddock?" she asks my brother, who is scraping what's left of his ice cream out of his cup.

"No, I wouldn't think he would, though the poor guy has a lot on his plate. He still has no staff at the manor, so the few people who do stay there aren't pleased," he says when he finishes his mouthful.

Mom nods her head, frowning. "We talked about it the other day. Pru and Al are working out there now that Ruby is back and running the candy store, and your father is going to help too. Maddock doesn't *really* need him, and until Regan can get a few more staff, he needs all the help he can get, especially while setting up the realm travel business. The manor will be the base for each jump, so it needs to be ready for an influx of people. We're predicting the realm travel is going to be very popular. Now that you're back, Tatiana, and the ice-cream shop is in such good hands, I might offer to help too. We have no commitments, and poor Regan is running on fumes with everything that is going on and being a single dad."

"How old are the twins now?" I ask Maddock, and he grins, his affection for them obvious. "Four, and they are little dynamos, on the go twenty-four seven. They go to a childcare place in town, but he doesn't like to leave them there very often. Pru watches them more often than not. That's why Al was running the candy store and they employed Jenna. I don't understand how someone can walk away from her own children."

My nose wrinkles at the reminder of Regan's ex. "I never liked that woman. There was just something about her that never sat right with me. Ruby felt the same way, but she never would have told him. She loves her brother and wanted to support him, but she and Susan never got along."

"The kids don't miss her from what I understand. I don't even think they really remember her. They are so happy to have Ruby home. They adore her, and they love having sleepovers at her cottage."

"I bet they are not the only ones!" I wink at him, and he blushes slightly. A huge smile crosses my face. I never would have thought I'd see the day where my brother blushes. Grabbing his hand, I give it a squeeze. "I am so happy for you both."

"Thank you," he says, the flush leaving his cheeks as he leans forward. "Now listen, there is something we need to talk about before you start jumping into all the renovations. I'm sure Ruby filled you in on what's been going on here, but were you using magic while you were away?"

I think about the question. When was the last time I used magic? "I can't remember the last time I used it," I answer, feeling a little disturbed, and he nods his head.

"Ruby was the same. We think it's part of the spell keeping you away. You need to be careful, though, because Ruby just about killed herself teleporting before she stretched her magic muscles. I need you to think carefully before you attempt anything."

The little chimes ring again as the door to the ice-cream store opens, and Ruby's mom, Pru, walks in, looking elegant and put together, as usual. Her arms are stretched wide in that *give me a hug* gesture, so I stand up, and she folds me into her body, her signature fragrance of violets surrounding me.

"Tatiana, you beautiful girl, it's so good to have you home." She pulls back, patting me on the cheek and giving me a wink. "Just what the town needs, another sassy lady to get it back on its feet." She takes the seat Dad vacated. "And did I hear Maddock say you needed to practice your magic? I have just the thing," she says, clapping her hands in glee. "We're having a Halloween haunted house and maze out at the manor to bring in some more tourists."

My mom frowns at her. "But you don't have a cornfield out there."

"Not yet, we don't. If Meadow returned, I would be asking her to help out, being so in tune with nature as she is, but beggars can't be choosers, so how about you, Tatiana? Go stay at the manor free of charge and help grow the cornfield. Just putting in a little magic every day will help you build up your stamina, and we will have a maze ready by Halloween." She gives my mom a look I don't quite understand. "Regan needs some help organizing the haunted house, so when Tatiana is not here, she can do that. The bonus is she gets to see Ruby, who's there all the time for meals." She turns to Maddock. "You need that one to learn how to cook. She can make exquisite candies, but ask her to boil pasta, and she can burn water."

He shrugs. "Why should she? The food at the manor is great." He winks at her, and she sighs in exasperation.

"That's because I'm the cook at the moment."

He laughs, leans over, and gives her a kiss on the cheek. "I know. That's why it's so good."

"Thanks for the offer to stay, Pru, but I'm sure Mom and Dad have room for me at their place," I say to her before turning to Mom. "You haven't turned my room into a craft room or anything, have you?" I ask jokingly.

The frown on Mom's face disappears, and a sheepish grin replaces it. "Well, actually, it is being used for storage. Your father has gotten into this game called Warhammer, and his model building supplies and table are in your room. I think staying out at the manor and helping Regan is a fabulous idea. Ruby and Maddock practically live there too, so it will give you all time to reconnect." She and Pru share a secret smile, but I've learned to ignore them over the years. Those women are always scheming something.

"Well, as long as you're okay with it. I'm not going to turn down a fancy room at the manor, especially if Pru is cooking."

"I am, but Regan has a few chefs coming to interview soon, as well as staff for other positions—supernaturals from other towns who are looking for a new change. It will be nice to have some new blood. That reminds me, I must go and talk to Lucas about approving more housing if they decide to stay." She stands up. "Maddock, can you give her a lift out there now? I will call Regan and tell him she's coming." He nods his head, and in a rush of violets and fabric, she leaves, waving goodbye over her shoulder.

Leaning back against the booth, I let out a big sigh. "I may have been gone a while, but some things never change. She's just as much of a hurricane now as she was before."

Mom just smiles as she watches her disappear into thin air. Ruby told me we can't teleport from inside the buildings anymore, since they warded them all after Candy Connection was broken into a few weeks ago.

Maddock stands up and stretches, bends down and gives Mom a kiss, and then pulls his keys out of his pocket. "Shall we go?" He picks up my backpack from the floor, hauling it onto his shoulder.

"Come out to the manor tonight after closing up, and we'll have a drink and discuss plans," I suggest to Mom, and she nods while wrapping her arms around me again.

"Love you, baby. Glad you're back."

As I follow Maddock out to the car, he turns to me. "Be grateful Mom and Pru are distracted by the mess the town is in. Imagine if they didn't have anything to concentrate on, and their attention was turned to all of us."

I shudder at the thought of their meddling being aimed in my direction. "When you put it like that, this drama with the island isn't such a bad thing."

We both laugh and get into his truck, and he heads in the direction of the manor.

CHAPTER
Three

Regan

S itting behind the desk in my office at the manor, I survey the mountain of crap that is sitting on it. There are papers piled so high they are listing slightly to the side. Where did it all come from? Surely this can't be the crap that Julie dealt with?

I lean back, and a huge sigh leaves my mouth, blowing one of the pages toward the floor. I watch as it slowly drifts down, like a feather on the breeze. It comes to a gentle stop just in front of the door where a pair of steel-toed boots prevent it from going any farther.

Looking up at the owner of the boots, I growl, "Why did you have to fire Julie, damn it? Look at all of this. I have resumes coming out of my ears and so many expressions of interest in the realm tours—tours that aren't even finalized! How am I going to get the time to do all of this and run Mom's damn haunted house and maze?"

Ruby just lifts one of her eyebrows and flips her pink hair behind her shoulder before putting her hands on her hips. Uh-oh. I brace myself for the tirade.

"May I remind you that woman left marks on your children?" she says, tapping one steel-toed boot. "She was rude and intolerable and had some stupid ideas for the manor, our manor, so yes, I fired her."

Shaking my head, I blow out another sigh, causing another sheet of paper to float off to join the first as I lean back in my chair. "No! No, you're right, I'm sorry. It's just with the lack of staff, I'm feeling overwhelmed, and she did take care of some of the less important things."

She smiles and bends down, picking up both pieces of paper before walking over to the desk. "I know, and that's why I'm here. I just dropped Tatiana at Dreamy Delights, and I have all afternoon to help you sort things out."

"God yes," I say, standing up and going around to give her a hug. "I'm sorry. You're back from Italy, so the trip was successful and Tatiana's back. That's great. Maddock will be pleased. He missed her as much as I missed you."

"Yeah, he was excited. He headed over there as soon as I called and told him I was back."

"No backlash issues from the spell?" I'm curious to know. Ruby's mentor died of a heart attack just after the ladies performed the spell. Mom thinks it was due to the consequences and feels guilty over it, but Ruby brushed it off, saying he wasn't very good at looking after his health anyway.

An angry look crosses Ruby's face. "When we went back to the apartment Tatiana shared with her boyfriend Marco, we found him buried balls deep in someone who wasn't Tatiana. He swears he's never done it before, so maybe it's part of the consequences." She shrugs but doesn't look too concerned. "I'm pretty sure she is devastated but putting on a brave face. They have been together for a while now."

I cringe at the image her words bring. "God, thanks for that, Ruby, I didn't need those images going through my mind."

She laughs at my discomfort. "Tatiana is home, and she's making things right with her family unit at the moment, so I'm all yours for the next couple of hours. What do we need to do?"

Going back behind the desk, I hand her a pile of resumes. "Can you help me go through these? Julie was in charge of this before, but she said no one was suitable."

She looks at the vast pile I just handed her skeptically. "No one?" She sounds doubtful.

"Yeah, that's why I thought I would go through them again. I need chefs, housekeeping, front of house staff, and groundskeepers. I also need a new stable master. Jandar's been helping, but he has his own horses to worry about."

She pulls up a spare chair onto the other side of the desk and sits down. "Let's do this."

We spend the next two hours poring over all the resumes until we have two piles—one for potentials, and the other for rejects. We're just finishing up when a knock on the doorframe draws our attention. Maddock strolls in and gives my sister a big kiss on the mouth. It's like they haven't seen each other for days. Oh, hang on, they haven't. She's been in Italy dragging his sister home. Speaking of his sister, she's standing just outside the doorway. Her eyes are on Maddock and Ruby, so I can study her quickly without looking like I'm staring.

She's really grown into herself. When she left, she still had that teenage girl look about her, but now she's all woman. Her cheekbones are more pronounced, and with her chestnut hair pulled up into a ponytail, her neck looks long and elegant, lending her a classic Audrey Hepburn style. Her blue eyes sparkle with delight, and her full, plump lips are turned up in a smile as she watches her brother and my sister.

I let my eyes quickly trail down her figure, hoping that they keep her attention a little longer. Her breasts are full, and her waist is trim, flaring back out into womanly hips. She is not the skinny beanpole I remember, and her legs make me think about what they would feel like wrapped around my waist as I drill into her.

What the fuck? Where did that thought come

from? God, I haven't had regular sex in years. Maybe that's the problem. I need to do something about that.

I discreetly adjust my cock and will it to go back down, thinking about other things to help. *Kadir's dirty socks, cleaning up Kady's vomit last time she got the stomach flu, my ex-wife. Ah, that works.*

"Well, don't just stand there, come on in," I tell her while getting up and going over to her. "Ignore the mush-fest, they are always like that. Kadir is grossed out by it, but Kady's worryingly fascinated." I grab her by the hand and pull her past the door and into my arms. "Tatiana, I'm so glad you're here. I desperately need a buffer." I swirl her around before pulling back and smacking a kiss on her cheek. "And such a pretty buffer you've become too." She feels good in my arms, all soft and round. Her pretty pink cheeks and the sparkle in her eyes make my stomach lurch like it hasn't done in years. *Crap, what were those thoughts again?* I step back quickly, putting some space between us.

"Regan, it's good to see you." Her smile drops, and the light in her eyes dims. "I'm sorry about what happened between you and Susan."

Yep, that does it.

Feeling uncomfortable, I move behind my desk. "It is what it is. I have two wonderful kids because of it, so it wasn't all a waste." I grab the picture of the twins I have on the desk and hand it to her. She takes it, and her face lights up again. "God, they could be you and Ruby all over again."

Ruby and Maddock finish their damn smooching,

and she decides to join the conversation. "Nah, we never got into as much mischief as they do," Ruby chimes in.

Maddock and Tatiana exchange glances before simultaneously bursting into laughter. "Are you serious?" Maddock asks, wrapping his arm around her waist and looking down at her. "You two were always up to no good, and Tatiana and I would get dragged into whatever schemes you cooked up. Mom swears you two were responsible for a few early gray hairs."

"Remember that time—" Tatiana gets cut off when Ruby lunges at her and wraps a hand around her mouth.

"Now, now, no need to bring up old memories," she says, then scrunches up her nose in disgust and pulls her hand away. "Gross, Tatiana." She wipes her hand on her pants as the rest of us chuckle.

Maddock throws himself down in the chair Ruby was sitting in and pulls her down into his lap. Shaking my head at the two of them, I get up and grab a chair out of the corner and pull it over for Tatiana.

She smiles at me as she sits down, and it really does light up her face. "Thank you, Regan."

"Did Pru call you, Regan?" Maddock asks me, moving Ruby's pastel pink hair out of his eyes.

Dragging my gaze away from Tatiana, I give myself a mental shake. *Get it together, man.* "No. Was she going to?"

Maddock just laughs, but Tatiana blushes as he continues. "She has cooked up another scheme."

Leaning back in my chair, I fold my arms. "Now, why doesn't that surprise me? The last one ended with them all crashing at the manor drunk and stoned after creating that spell for the girls."

Tatiana's eyes widen. "Stoned? My mom?" She sounds doubtful.

Maddock laughs. "You better believe it. Now that marijuana has been made legal here, the coven ladies occasionally indulge. Mom was talking about making marijuana ice cream, for fuck's sake."

Her eyes widen, and then a curious expression crosses her face. "Hmm, I really should find a recipe for it. I'm sure it would sell like crazy.

Maddock shakes his head before turning back to me. "This scheme involves you. Well, kind of. She knows how swamped you are with being short-staffed and the realm tours, and now you have this Halloween party to organize too."

I slump down in my chair, groaning. "Dude, don't remind me. I swear I need to find a replicating spell and use it on myself so that there are more of me."

Ruby sits up straighter on Maddock's lap. "I could probably do that. I found an old spell book in the attic of Mom and Dad's place. It has all sorts of cool spells. I'll check it out."

"How would that even work?" Tatiana asks with surprise.

"I'm not sure. I'll do some research and maybe call Nana? She may have some answers."

A shudder runs down my spine at the mention of Nana, and I can see Tatiana and Maddock are similarly affected.

Ruby laughs. "You pansies! Poor Nana."

A sheepish look crosses Maddock's face. "Ruby, you know we love your nana, but the woman is so damn powerful it's scary sometimes."

I rub the back of my neck. "Yeah, Ruby, for some reason, it never seems to bother you, but the woman practically sparks sometimes."

"Anyway," Maddock says, returning our focus to him, "Pru has sacrificed my sister here." He gestures to Tatiana. "Offered her up with the bribe of staying here in return for helping you. Oh, and she also gets to stretch her magic muscles by growing the cornfield, so she doesn't do a Ruby and just about kill herself by accident while using big magic before she's ready."

I look at her in surprise. "You haven't been using your magic either?"

She shakes her head in shame. "No, Marco was human and anti-supernatural, so I hid my magic from him to start with, and then it was like I forgot I had magic too."

Ruby nods. "I think it's a side effect from the spell. I knew I had magic, but every time I tried to use it, it would go haywire, so I just stopped using it."

Maddock looks at me, raising an eyebrow. "What do you say, man? You help my sister out, and she will help you."

I look at Tatiana, whose big, doe-like eyes are staring at me hopefully, and I blow out a breath. "If you can take care of this damn Halloween party for me, that would remove a huge weight off my shoulders. I assume you're going to be working at the ice-cream store too. Are you going to be able to handle both?"

She smiles, creating a gorgeous glow, and I have to discreetly adjust myself again. *Jesus, what is wrong with me?*

"I promise I can do both no problem. The ice-cream store is going to close for a week or two and have some renovations like the candy store had. Mom is coming out later tonight to get that started, but the Halloween party and haunted house is a piece of cake. I'll make a few phone calls and organize some decorations and food and things. I can work on the cornfield as well. Don't worry, we'll have this nailed down in no time."

"If you can manage all that, I'll kiss your feet, and with Ruby taking care of the interviews and new hires, I can concentrate on the realm tours."

Ruby sits up straight on Maddock's lap. "What? Why me?" she questions.

"You did a great job sorting through resumes, so you might as well keep going, and it is still half your business too."

She mumbles under her breath but agrees when Maddock offers to help.

Tatiana laughs at them and nods her head. "Regan, I need a favor too," she tells me quietly like she's embarrassed to ask.

Leaning forward, I nod for her to continue.

"I need some new flavors for the ice-cream shop, and I thought if we could offer something new that's never been seen before, it would attract attention. Can I join you when you go into the realms and see if I can find a new fruit or something?"

My heart starts to race at the thought of spending more time with her. Running my hands through my hair, I lean back against my chair again. I can't stop fidgeting. What is wrong with me? I internally roll my eyes at myself. It's not like I'm a teenage boy.

Get it together. You're a grown man with two kids and an ex-wife.

Looking up, I realize I must be taking too long to answer, because all three of them are looking at me weirdly.

Shaking my head, I apologize. "Sorry, I'm not getting a lot of sleep. I zoned out for a second." Pitying looks cross their faces, but I ignore them. "I don't see any problem with that. Why don't you talk to Galan? He might be able to make a suggestion about what's available in the fae realm, and the mayor might be able to suggest something from the vampire realm. I'm doing realm visits at the beginning of next week to finalize everything, so that gives you some time to settle in. Sound good?"

She nods enthusiastically, and a tendril of hair slips from her ponytail. She pushes it behind her ear, making me think about nibbling on it, before turning to Ruby. "Can I borrow your laptop? I need to get myself one, but I want to get started on plans for the haunted house so that when Mom comes by later, I can work on the shop."

Ruby starts to reply, but I interrupt by standing up. "I've got a spare," I tell her, going to a cabinet and pulling it out. "Here, you can use this for as long as you want. Just give me a minute, and I'll go grab a key for your room from the front desk." When I pass her the computer, our fingers brush, and my cock roars back to life. Our eyes lock, and a blush colors her cheeks again. A swirling breeze floats through the room, bringing her perfume to my nose, and I inhale deeply.

Tearing my eyes away from her, I rush from the office to clear my head while still planning on putting her room as close to mine as possible.

CHAPTER
Four

Tatiana

"Yeah." Ruby fist-bumps the air, drawing my attention away from the doorway that Regan practically ran through. My fingertips tingle from where I brushed his when he handed me the laptop. Dirty thoughts run through my mind, wondering if my clit would also tingle if he put those same fingertips there.

Crap, Ruby's talking, stop having dirty thoughts about her brother. The man's clearly exhausted and has two kids, so there is no way he's interested in you.

I hear my name being called, and when I look up, I find Ruby eyeing me suspiciously. "Are you okay? You didn't hear a word I just said."

"Jet lag," I blurt out, shaking my head. "Sorry, what were you saying?"

She seems to believe me and starts to blabber again. "I was just saying how great it is to have the four musketeers back together again. With us all working together, I'm sure we can get Regan organized and the manor thriving again."

My brother has the cheesiest grin on his face as he watches her. It is so lovely to see them together and happy. A little bit of jealousy pokes me in the chest, but I push it back down. Marco obviously wasn't meant to be, and really, what was I thinking? I'm a witch, and he's anti-supernatural. It was never going to work. Maybe the spell did me a favor.

"It's nice to be home," I agree. "I am excited about fixing up the ice-cream shop, and Halloween really is one of my favorite holidays, so I'm eager to turn the mansion into a haunted house. It's going to be so much fun." Just then, Regan rushes back in, breathing heavily.

"What did you do? Run all the way?" my brother asks him.

He leans against the doorframe and gasps for breath. "Yes. I saw Julie walking through the front door, so I grabbed the key and bolted as soon as I heard her call my name."

Ruby jumps off Maddock's lap. "What is that bitch doing back here? I'm going to give her a piece of my mind." She hurries back the way Regan came.

Regan turns to Maddock, a pleading look on his face. "Please stop her. I don't need any more trouble. Just see what Julie wants and deal with it, then get Ruby back here and make sure she organizes those interviews. I need more staff, or I will have to hire her back."

Maddock chuckles. "Sure thing. Sort out Tatiana, and I'll worry about Ruby."

Regan looks relieved. "Thanks, man, I owe you one." Maddock hurries after Ruby as Regan gestures to me. "Shall we head to your room?"

Nodding, I move out of his way and allow him to lead. Putting the laptop under my arm, I grab my backpack from outside the door, haul it over my shoulder, and follow after him. He turns back and notices the pack and stops to take it from me. I let him. It's nice to see manners on a man. So many of them don't have them these days. Marco certainly wouldn't have done it.

We don't go very far before he stops at a door and swipes a card through a slot next to it. "All our doors are magic-proof. It just protects the guest a little bit more and gives them peace of mind. We also stopped teleporting in and out after the candy store was broken into. The foyer is the only place you can tele-port to in the manor," he informs me as he pushes the door open before stopping and gesturing at the door across from us. "That's mine. All the rooms are soundproof, and they know not to bother guests, but if Kadir and Kady get in your way, just let me know."

He continues into the room. "You're welcome to order all meals from the kitchen as well if you want, but I am warning you, it's still a bit hit and miss until we get some more staff, which Ruby will hopefully take care of in the next week or so."

"Don't worry about me," I tell him, following him into the room. "I can always make my own meals if you don't mind me using the kitchen. I'll be fine. I wouldn't want to make extra trouble for you." Looking around the room, I don't notice when he puts my backpack on the ground, so I walk straight into it. I hit my shins and tumble forward into Regan, who also gets knocked off balance, and we both fall onto the bed. My heartbeat pounds in my ears, and my breath rushes out of my lungs as I find myself sprawled across his body. A breath of air leaves his lungs as he supports my full weight as I land on him, his hand reaching up to hold my hips.

My ponytail is draped across my face and in my mouth as we come to a stop. As I reach up to pull it away, my body connects even more with Regan's, making me pause. His long, lean muscles are hard against my softer ones. My breasts are squished against his chest, and as I look up into his eyes, his disheveled reddish hair and the heat sparkling in his green gaze gives him a devilish look.

"Oops, sorry," I say, and his eyebrow rises.

"Oops indeed," he agrees, and I squirm to get off him, but our tangled limbs and the softness of the bed makes it a little tricky. I wiggle a bit more, and he grunts as my knee connects with his inner thigh. "Stop, Tatiana. Just stop for a second," Regan pleads with me, his grip on my hips tightening.

I come to a stop, wondering what's wrong and worried that I have hurt him in some way. That's when I realize precisely what's wrong. Our hips are now flush with each other, and there is no mistaking that bulge.

He takes a couple of deep breaths and looks down at me with embarrassment in his gaze. "I'm sorry. It's been a long time since a beautiful woman wiggled around on top of me." A wry grin curves his lips. "Having twins doesn't exactly make having a sex life easy, especially when you're a single dad."

Biting my lip, I make a split-second decision that may cost me a lot, but fuck it. I slide my body up and cover his mouth with mine, gently tasting those plump lips that I've always wondered about.

He doesn't react, and my heart plummets. I pull back, but in a flurry of action, he rolls and pins me before kissing me like he's been starved of oxygen and I'm his only air supply. It is glorious.

Heat streaks straight to my core, and he grinds his thick, jean-clad length against it, ramping up the intensity. My hands wind through his hair, the perfect length for me to grab hold of, and our tongues wrestle for dominance. A flash of magic streams out from both of us, the shockwave dragging our mouths apart, but no words are exchanged, nor is it acknowledged in our frenzy.

He pulls back and looks at me for permission to continue. He must see my acceptance and my desire for more in my eyes, because he starts placing kisses down my neck toward my cleavage. His light stubble rubs against my skin, creating a subtle contrast to his gentle caresses. His mouth leaves my body, and he grips the hem of my shirt when childish voices yell, "Dad!"

A look of panic crosses his face. As we both sit up

on the bed, our eyes shoot to the still open door. He jumps up like he's been shot out of a gun and straightens himself out, adjusting the bulge in his jeans. "I'm so sorry, Tatiana," he apologizes without even looking at me. "I shouldn't have taken advantage like that." Before I know it, he's pulling the door closed behind him and leaving me all worked up.

Flopping back like a starfish, I blow out a huge breath and will my hormones to settle. Wow, making out with Regan has me more worked up than sex with Marco ever did.

Rolling over, I check out my room a little more. The bed has already been tested and approved, so I move on to the small seating area. There's a comfy-looking sofa and a coffee table with a TV on the wall in front of it. To one side is what looks like a built-in wardrobe, so I grab my backpack and toss it in there. I will deal with that later.

Looking at the time on my phone, I realize I still have a little time before Mom finishes at the ice-cream store, so I decide to take a shower and wash off all of the grime from traveling.

I'm sure I can get my shit together if I actually feel like a human being once again. The Halloween plans can wait a little while longer.

An hour later, I'm dressed and drying my long hair with a towel when Mom knocks on my door. Opening it, I greet her with another long hug. I seriously need a lot more of those to make up for all the ones I missed out on.

"Let me just do my hair, and we'll go down to the bar and grab a drink and talk about renovations." She waits while I quickly brush and throw my damp hair into a ponytail. Grabbing my laptop, I pull the door closed behind me, and then we head down to the bar area of the manor.

It's deserted when we get there. The only person around is the man behind the counter polishing a glass. He puts it down and comes to take our order. We tell him what we want and go take a seat.

I power up the computer and open a new document. "Okay, Mom, let's start with the inside of the store."

She nods her head and smiles, placing her hand on my knee. "Tatiana, you can do whatever you want to it. It's yours now," she tells me, a gentle smile on her face. "It's what we've always wanted, so any decision you make is fine with me."

"Great, so we need to talk to Gerald and Bram about everything we'll need—new booths, new flooring, a cozy sitting area with a fire and bookshelves, and a new counter stretching the length of the store. I also want room for a liquid nitrogen bottle and stand mixer, and I also want a stainless steel metal slab to make stir-fried ice cream."

She holds her hand up. "Hang on! Stir-fried ice cream? What on earth is that?"

I stop typing my list and turn to her. "When I was in Thailand, I saw this really cool way of making ice cream. They pour the liquid onto an ice-cold slab. The liquid is then scraped and chopped until it's mixed to the right consistency. To serve it, they scrape it into rolls and serve them in a cup. It's another fun way to serve ice cream, and we can make different flavored liquids and add other mix-ins and things."

"And the liquid nitrogen?" she inquires.

"Hang on," I reply, and then I open the YouTube browser and search liquid nitrogen ice cream and show her a video of it being made. "I'll have to do some experimenting, but I think we can make it into different shapes by dropping it into liquid nitrogen. Like if we drip it in drop by drop, it will be little round ball shapes. I'm hoping we can maybe come up with others too." I then pull up the video of stir-fried ice cream and show her that one as well. "And this is the last thing I want to do." I show her the classic cold marble slab, where the ice cream has a whole heap of additional toppings added and mixed in.

She blows out a breath and leans back on the couch. "I guess I really have gotten out of touch," she mutters, her brows furrowing. "Maybe if I had kept up to date with all the new offerings, we wouldn't be struggling."

"Oh, Mom, no." Shifting down on the couch, I wrap an arm around her shoulders. "It's not your fault. None of it is. Remember, there's a spell causing problems," I remind her. "That's something we're going to fix as soon as we can get all the girls back. Ruby and I will chase them all down if they don't come back by themselves. Let's get through this rebuild and the Halloween party for Regan, and then we'll go get them. I promise."

She nods, and I give her a squeeze before moving over. The guy from the bar finally delivers our cocktails. I give him a smile and say, "Thanks," but he just grunts and turns to the bar. *Huh, he's not very friendly.*

Turning to the drinks, I grab my mojito and take a sip. "You talked about marijuana-infused ice cream, so why don't we make a range of cocktail infused sorbets and ice creams as well? That should attract the adults who will also bring their kids."

Mom claps her hands in delight and reaches for her own drink. "I'm so excited about this. I can't wait to create the recipes." She stops suddenly and looks at me. "Unless you don't want me to? I did say it was your shop."

I just about snort my drink out of my nose. "Are you kidding me? Mom, I would love you to. I still have the haunted house to organize and a field of corn to grow. Not to mention I'm going into the realms with Regan to find us something new and interesting for our customers. If there's anything you want to help with, have at it."

CHAPTER
Five

Tatiana

Mom and I work on the designs and color scheme, as well as order the equipment we're going to need online.

Just as we finish, Dad arrives and grabs a seat on the opposite couch. He takes note of the glasses spread out on the table in front of us. "Been working hard, have we, ladies?" Dad asks, a laugh in his voice.

By now, Mom's pretty hammered, and she throws herself at him. "Oh, Phil, our baby is back, and she has amazing ideas." She squishes his cheeks between her hands, his mouth puckers up, and she smacks a kiss on it. "And she's going to make some amazing concoctions and people are going to love them."

He laughs and grabs her hands and pulls her down next to him. "That sounds great, but maybe we should slow down a little tonight."

"Phsss," she scoffs but settles with a smile on her face. My mom's a lightweight.

"Dad, did you find out who owns the land?" I ask, bringing his attention back to me.

A frown crosses his face. "I did actually. It's coven land and has been since Morbank Island was first settled. It was used for ceremonies, gatherings, and meetings. I think it will need a vote, but I can't see them not approving our plans, especially since it will revitalize the land and bring back joy, laughter, and love with all the families that will use it."

"That's perfect. I'll ask Pru to call a coven meeting so I can petition them to use it. Once we get their permission, we can finalize the plans for outside, but the inside is good to go," I say just as Maddock, Ruby, Pru, and Alistair walk into the bar.

"There you all are. We thought we'd all have dinner together since it's been so long since our families have been together," Pru announces. "Let's head to the Laughing Hamster. That way, no one has to cook. Where's Regan? I called him and told him about the plan." She looks around the room.

"We saw him earlier. He was dealing with Julie after she begged for her job back." Ruby huffs, rolling her eyes. "I think he's crazy, but whatever. He's pretty damn desperate, and she even apologized to the children. She's blaming her behavior on some family stress."

Just as she finishes speaking, two bundles of energy barrel into the room.

"Aunt Wuby!" the redheaded boy says.

"Uncle Maddy!" the girl shouts.

They launch themselves at my brother and Ruby, who quickly drop their hands to catch them. They both get swung around in a circle, and giggles ring out.

When they are both put down, it's Pru and Al's turn for the ritual. Alistair staggers when Kady jumps at him, one arm around her and one holding his heart. "Did you get bigger overnight?" he asks her with an incredulous look on his face. "I swear you're so much taller." He puts her down, and Kadir throws himself at him.

"What about me, Poppy? What about me?"

Alistair fake staggers and pretends to struggle to lift him. "Yes, you too. What have you been eating?" More giggles explode from the children until they see me. The laughter stops instantly, and curious looks cross their faces.

"Who are you?" Kadir asks while Kady sticks her thumb in her mouth. Their green eyes are filled with curiosity.

Before I can answer, however, Regan enters behind them with a frustrated look on his face. "What have I told you two about running in the manor?"

They both look sheepishly at the ground at his words, and together, "Sorry, Dad," comes out of their mouths. It's a little creepy, but Ruby and Regan used to do the same thing when they were young too.

"Guys, this is Uncle Maddock's sister, Tatiana."

Their eyes light up, and Kadir looks at Maddock with surprise on his face. "You have a sister too? Is she as much of a bum head as Kady is?"

All the adults laugh as Maddock crouches down to Kadir's level and pretends to whisper. "She was totally a bum head, but she is also my best friend, so I can forgive her for the bum head moments."

"Kadir, that's not very nice," Regan scolds. "Remember what I said about saying mean things?"

A smile curves my lips, and the warmth I feel is like nothing I've felt in a long time. Coming home was just what I needed. Both children turn to me and eye me warily, then they both hold out their hands for me to shake. Looking at Regan, I lift my eyebrow and smirk, and a proud smile crosses his face.

I step up and shake Kady's hand first and then Kadir's. "It's lovely to meet you both," I tell the angelic-looking, red-haired children who I'm almost sure have a devil streak a mile wide. "I've been friends with your dad and Aunt Ruby since we were younger than you guys."

Their eyes widen in amazement.

"Tatiana has come home to take over running the ice-cream shop for Miss Lucille. She's going to make it look all fancy and add some new kinds of treats to the menu," Regan informs them, and this time their eyes almost bug out of their heads as they both move closer, crowding me as rapid-fire questions pop out.

"What new things are you adding? You're not

getting rid of bubble gum, are you?" Kadir asks, looking worried.

"What new things are you going to do? The ice-cream store is my favorite," Kady tells me, speaking a little quieter than her normal voice.

"Hey," Ruby says with her hands on her hips, and a sheepish look crosses Kady's face.

"Second favorite," she quickly corrects, and then throws me an exaggerated wink that everyone can see. Again, all the adults laugh. Wow, these two are really something.

"Now that everyone's here, shall we head out?" Alistair asks, looking around. "How are we going to get there?"

"I'll drive," Regan offers. "The kids can't teleport yet, and maybe Tatiana should come with us."

"That's a great idea," Dad agrees. "We wouldn't want the same thing to happen to her that happened to Ruby. Until you've worked your magic a little more, let's stick to small things."

When we arrive at the Hamster, the parents are all there, having teleported. The evening is bleak and miserable with a fine drizzle in the air. We all rush from the car toward the portico to stay dry.

Maddock and Ruby followed us in Maddock's

truck. Maddock still wasn't ready for Ruby to tele-port, even though she claims to be back to full power, but it's a true testament to how she feels for him because she let him get away with his demands. She threatened it's the last time though.

Staring at the stained glass windows at the Hamster, I'm pleased to see them not looking quite as sad and dreary as Ruby told me they were, but I still send a small burst of magic into them as I walk by. That little bit of magic causes a slight pain in my temple, the shock stopping me in my tracks. My hand goes to my temple in an attempt to ease the pain, and Ruby rubs my arm as she walks by. "It gets easier. Just use a little bit at a time."

It's still early, and there are plenty of tables avail-able. A fire is lit in the fireplace, bringing a soothing warmth to the bar. That and the warm lighting, a stark contrast to the unpleasant weather outside. A waitress shows us to a table and leaves some menus, telling us she'd be back shortly to take our drink orders. The table is a chaotic mess of voices as everyone has different conversations while Kady and Kadir argue about who they are going to sit next to.

When it's eventually sorted, I find myself sitting next to Regan, with Kady on the other side, and then Maddock, Kadir, and Ruby. Facing us are our parents. The waitress comes back, and everyone places their drink orders before looking at the menu.

Conversation is pleasant, and I'm caught up on the gossip for the island. The children are busy with the colored pencils the waitress gave them, furiously coloring pictures of dragons and fairies and arguing over whose is better. I am consciously aware of Regan sitting next to me, his body heat acting as a furnace to my overactive mind. The kiss we shared in my bedroom earlier roars back into my thoughts like a freight train, and a wave of desire flows through my body.

What is happening? I feel such a pull toward him. I always thought he was a handsome man, but he was Susan's, and that was that. No other thought had ever crossed my mind. I don't do the cheating thing or pining from a distance.

"Do you have any ideas for the haunted house yet, Tatiana?" Pru asks me, nudging me out of my thoughts. Everyone at the table turns their attention to me, and I am grateful for the distraction.

"No, not yet. I haven't had a chance to think about it, but Mom and I were able to make decisions about the ice-cream store, so that's organized or will be as soon as we can speak to Gerald and Bram. I'm hoping to visit the realms with Regan, and after I do that, I'll work on the haunted house."

Pru nods her head in understanding. "You should start working with your magic as soon as possible, so you don't end up in the same situation as Ruby."

Ruby rolls her eyes in disgust. "You make one little teleporting mistake, and no one lets you hear the end of it."

"Mistake!" Pru screeches. "That little mistake almost cost you your life."

Al pats her hand. "Yes, and she was very sorry. She even admitted you were right. You need to let it go."

Pru huffs in response but lets the subject drop.

Josh chooses that moment to bring our drinks over to the table. "Look at this, the Miller and Crane families together again just like the old days. What an awesome sight." He sets the glasses of beer on the table and bestows kisses to the ladies and shakes hands with the men before returning to the bar to get the remainder of the drinks.

"In fact, I'm so happy to see it, the meals are on me tonight." Everyone tries to argue with him, but he won't hear it. "No, no, as far as I'm concerned, you are the starting lineup in the war against the darkness that surrounds the island, so we need to look after you. If you guys can get Estrella to come home, that would be awesome." A frown crosses his face. "Mom mopes around the studio. She has piles of fabric to sew together for quilts and bunches of paper to cut for quilling. I wanted her to make me coasters for the bar. That was weeks ago, and I still have no coasters." Frustration enters his voice. "She has even stopped advertising her craft classes. She's a mess and regrets telling Estrella that tattooing isn't a craft."

Wincing, I remember how she reacted when her mom said that tattooing wasn't art.

"She expected her to lose interest and focus on all the things she learned while growing up so she could take over the studio. And now, because of the spell, she has no way to apologize and invite her home.

She's driving Dad nuts, so to escape, he comes into the brewery and starts throwing his weight around, which is driving *me* nuts." The look of annoyance on Josh's face is amusing, and the table laughs and thanks him for his kindness.

"Send him out to the manor," Pru orders. "We will put him to work and keep him out of your hair."

A grateful look crosses his face. "Thanks, Pru. I might just do that. If I tell him it's an order from you, he can't argue with it." He shoots her a wink and heads back to the bar.

Conversation continues around us, but Regan leans close, and I feel like we're suddenly in our own bubble. His voice is low, and his breath on my ear sends a shiver down my spine. "I've temporarily rehired Julie. The trip to the realms will probably take a couple of days. I'm allowing one day for each realm we visit. She should be able to take care of things at the manor while I'm gone."

My eyes are drawn to his lips, distracting me. The thought of kissing him again sends another pulse of desire through my body. Dragging my eyes away, I tune back in.

"The kids will stay with Mom and Dad while we're gone. We'll be going into the fae realm first, then the vampire and shifter realms. Barring any trouble, and as long as they give the go-ahead, we should be ready to start realm tours just after Halloween."

I take a long swallow of my wine before replying, "That sounds great. I think I'll go find Galan and ask him about what I might discover in the fae realm. That will give me a head start, and I won't be dragging you down timewise searching for things. Order me the brisket with cornbread and potato salad when the waitress comes back, will you?" Standing up quickly, I walk away before I can do anything silly.

As I approach the bar, a group of girls comes into the Hamster. I don't pay attention to them, but I do notice their loud, obnoxious voices are irritating. Ignoring them, I approach the back corner wine bar, looking for Galan. Rounding the corner to the storage area, I find him and Josh wrapped around each other, sharing an applause-worthy kiss.

Jesus, I walked away from Regan in the hope that the desire would leave, but seeing these two gorgeous men embracing each other just ramps it back up. I fan my face while clearing my throat to get their attention.

They break apart, looking a little dazed, and I feel slightly guilty and jealous.

"Sorry to interrupt. I was hoping I could speak to Galan, but I can come back," I apologize, but Josh waves it off. "No, don't be silly. We shouldn't be distracted during working hours, but damn, the man's hot, can you blame me?" He waves his hand, gesturing in Galan's direction.

"No." I shake my head. "If he was mine, I would climb him like a tree," I reply honestly, and a light pink blush heats the fae's face.

"Go on, be off with you," he tells Josh, shooing him back toward the bar.

"What can I do for you, Tatiana?" Galan has a gentle smile on his face and is open and warm. Josh really is a lucky man.

"I was wondering if you could tell me a little about the fae realm. Regan is going in a few days to settle the realm tours, and I'm going with him to source ingredients for new flavors of ice cream. I thought if you could tell me what's available, it might save me a little time."

"Hmm, yes, I could think of some ideas. When you're finished with dinner, why don't you come find me? I'll sit down and tell you about a few things and the best places to find them."

A huge grin crosses my face. "That would be great, thank you." I turn to head back to the table but see Ruby with a drink at the bar talking to Josh, so I walk over to them. They are both eyeing the group of girls I noticed when I first got up.

"What's going on?" I ask as I slide onto one of the bar stools. Ruby's nose wrinkles in disgust, and Josh has a frown on his face.

"That's the group of girls I was telling you about. The twins are Julie and Jenna Hart. Jenna works at Candy Connection with me. She's a hard worker, and Dad likes her, but she seems to loathe me—probably because I fired Julie from the manor. That's the other one. She is all over Regan all the time and was horrible to the children. I can't believe Regan rehired her."

I glance at Ruby. She looks like a dark storm waiting to unleash its fury on the world.

"Desperate times call for desperate measures, Ruby," Josh reminds her gently. "The one with the chestnut hair is Sheree. She's the one who was with Maddock. We are sure she's a supe but can't figure out what. We think she may be masking," Josh continues. "The Asian girl is Mia, she's been dating Taylor, and Minnie is the dirty blonde who has been trying to date Cullen, but I'm pretty sure she's part of the reason he is still out of town, avoidance being the keyword."

"I can't believe she has the nerve to show her face in this place. She's like a bad smell that you can't get rid of," Ruby grumbles in disgust. As we watch, Sheree gets up and walks over to the table, and Ruby straightens in alarm. "What the fuck?" she exclaims and starts to get up, but Josh grabs her and holds tight.

"Settle down! Just watch what happens."

Sheree sidles up to Maddock and puts her hand on his shoulder. He turns with a smile on his face, but when he realizes who it is, he shrugs her hand off. We can't hear what is said, but the visual makes it very clear. The smile on her face drops after his response. His face is all growly, and he has his Mad Maddock look on. I wouldn't want to be that girl. She needs to walk away now. She takes the hint and slinks back to her table where the other girls surround her, their heads close as they ask questions. She shakes her head, wearing a sad expression on her face before it quickly changes to scheming.

"You still haven't found out what they are?" Josh asks, wiping down the already clean bar.

Ruby shakes her head. "No, damn it, I've been so busy. They have to be masking themselves somehow. They must be supes. Maddock was always affected when she was near until he took the potion. I need to get to the bottom of this. I'll ask Taylor to look into it for me."

"Be careful with Taylor. He may be compromised too," Josh warns. "Cole might be the one to ask. He doesn't seem to be affected by any of them. I'll let him know to come see you next time he's here."

We watch as one of the blonde twins gets up.

"That's Julie," Ruby growls, and I sit up a little straighter. She heads over to our table and places her hand on Regan's shoulder. I can't hear what is being said, but the wave of jealousy that flows through me is enough to get me moving. I hurry back to the table and sit down in my seat before she can take it.

"I can't thank you enough for rehiring me," I hear her coo to Regan. "Is there anything I can do to thank you? Maybe take you to dinner or buy you a drink or something?"

Yeah, I bet there is 'something' you could do, I think, rolling my eyes, jealousy burning in my veins.

"Now that you are his employee again, I'm not sure that would be appropriate," I tell her just as the waitress delivers our dinner.

"How about always being punctual and working your hardest? I'm sure that will go a long way toward thanking him," Pru suggests with a look of irritation on her face. It seems like someone else is not ready to forgive and forget.

"Yes, if you will excuse us," Mom says as Ruby returns to the table, glaring at Julie. "We're celebrating our families being back together. You can see Regan at work." Mom's tone is dismissive and annoyed, and she's glaring back at the table with the other girls. That's right, Sheree was horrible to Mom when she was working for her.

Julie smiles at Regan, ignoring everyone else. The girl's got balls, I'll give her that. "Of course, enjoy your meal, Regan, and I will see you at work." She waves goodbye to him and walks away.

"I don't like her," Kadir says a little too loudly. "She's mean, and she lies."

Regan reaches over and ruffles his head. "I know, buddy. It's only for a little while until Aunt Ruby can do some interviews."

Ruby picks up her knife and fork and points the knife at him. "They are all scheduled. By the time you finish your realm visits, we should be good to go."

A massive sigh of relief escapes him, and I watch as his shoulders relax as some of the tension leaves his body. He reaches over and grabs the hand pointing at him and places a kiss on it. "Thank you." He's not quick enough to avoid the knife though, and she slices into his hand.

Ruby looks shocked and quickly grabs a napkin, wrapping it around his rapidly bleeding palm. "Jesus, what did you go and do that for?" she grumbles and says a quick incantation. When she pulls the napkin away, his hand is all healed.

He smiles. "All fixed, nothing to worry about." The conversation moves on, but I watch as Ruby slyly tucks the bloody napkin into her handbag.

Hmm, I'm going to have to corner my bestie and ask what the hell is going on.

CHAPTER
Six

Tatiana

Dinner is a relaxed and enjoyable affair. Dad talks to Pru about the coven space and what we'd like to do with it. She thinks it's a fabulous idea but insists it is a coven project, and coven funds or magic will be used to do what needs to be done.

"Once interviews are out of the way for the manor and it is fully staffed again, I'll call a full coven meeting," she announces. "That will allow everyone to express what things they would like to see done in the space. Then the responsibility won't all be on you, Tatiana, but it will still attract people into both the candy and ice-cream stores."

"That's actually a better idea than I had. I wasn't sure how I was going to manage that on top of the things I'm doing at the manor and the renovations to the ice-cream store," I say, grateful to have that taken out of my hands.

"So do you think there was any backlash from the spell for you, Tatiana?" Al asks, taking another sip of his beer. The table falls into an awkward silence, and he looks around. "Sorry, did I say something wrong?"

Glancing at the children, I can see they are not paying attention, so I explain what happened with Marco. I gaze around the room, unable to look anyone in the eye, and I notice that the table of girls is listening to what I just said. My cheeks heat with embarrassment as I realize they heard me tell everyone I wasn't exciting enough for my boyfriend to keep it in his pants. Putting my shoulders back, I look at my family and friends.

"But to be honest, I'm not all that upset. It brought me home to all of you." The tension eases, and the conversation turns to other things.

While the children have ice-cream sundaes for dessert, I sit with an Irish coffee while Galan tells me about the different fresh produce available in the fae realm. I take plenty of notes so that I don't forget anything. He has some great suggestions and tells me most things can be found in the large produce market in the main city of Faerie. By the time we leave the Hamster, I am full of ideas.

The drive back to the manor is quiet, and even though it isn't far, both children fall asleep. I help Regan by carrying Kady up to their suite. That way, he doesn't have to make two trips.

After we tuck them into their beds, we leave the door open a crack and go out to his living area.

"Thanks. I don't like to use a spell to carry the other up because they get disoriented and freak out if they wake." He smiles gratefully at me. The tension in his body from before has been replaced by sheer exhaustion. He looks like he is about to collapse.

"You're welcome. I'm going to go, you look exhausted," I tell him, heading to the door.

"Everything has finally caught up to me. Just knowing the staff interviews are scheduled is a huge weight off my shoulders, although I would prefer to be here for them. I don't trust Julie not to interfere, and I'd rather be able to keep an eye on her."

"I think Ruby is on top of that," I assure him. "She has a scheme in the works."

He rolls his eyes with a rueful smile. "I'm not sure if I'm relieved or worried."

Smiling at his comment, I wave and cross the hall to my room. Pulling out my card to swipe open my door, I notice it's open a crack. That's strange. I could have sworn I pulled it closed when Mom and I went and had a drink. Putting my key card back into my pocket, I push it open and reach around to turn on a light. I step in slowly and look around, but I can't see anyone. Maybe housekeeping left it open when they did turn down.

Placing my laptop bag on the bed, I notice a rose resting on my pillow. The green stem and blood-red petals are a stark contrast against the white sheets. I bring it to my nose, and the fragrance is strong and heady to my senses. What a beautiful thing for housekeeping to do. Looking around for somewhere to put it, I decided to give my magic another try. I hold out my hand and conjure up a little crystal bud vase. Simple and elegant, it's a slight weight in my hand as it appears. I feel another twinge of pain, but it's not too bad. Baby steps.

Going into the bathroom, I fill it with water and place the rose inside before putting it on the bedside table.

As I walk over to the window, I notice the moon is bright in the sky, shining down on the wide-open expanse of grass in front of the manor. Quite often, the manor horses are paddocked in this vast space, but for the sake of the maze, they have been moved to a paddock at the back of the manor. The grass shimmers brightly in the moonlight before being shrouded by shadows of the orchard on one side and the large forest—where Ruby's guesthouse is—on the other.

Making a quick decision, I leave my room, firmly pulling the door closed behind me this time. I head to the elevator and make my way down to the foyer. The desk is illuminated by a lamp, and I can see a shadow of someone manning the counter, but I don't stop to see who it is.

I hurry through the lobby, out the double doors, and down the steps, then I cross the gravel driveway before stopping at the edge of the expanse of grass. The air is still wet from the drizzle, cold and damp with every breath I take. I pull my coat up around my neck to keep the water from dripping down my back.

A shadow passes overhead, and I look up to see wispy clouds drift across the moon. Strange. It was clear before, but the wind is picking up, and I can see thicker clouds blowing toward us. I need to get this done quickly before the storm blows in.

Pru and Regan mentioned that they wanted the maze in this area, close to the manor and easily accessible to the driveway. Then people can do both the maze and the hayride without having to move too far. The hayride is going to stop right in front and pick people up then take them on a trip through the orchard before circling around and dropping them back off. We can set up a warm cider hut and maybe some roasted nuts or something to sell as well.

Concentrating on the ground, I think about a cornfield, visualizing little round golden kernels of corn sown into the ground beneath the grass. Sending out a gentle pulse of magic, I watch as the green light flows across the field. A drop of sweat lands on my cheek as it drips from my forehead, the strain from holding the magic bringing a sheen to my brow. Grunting with the pressure, I grit my teeth as my magic continues to creep slowly across the area.

As my breath starts to labor, and the tension becomes almost too much to bear, the green light reaches the far edge. Letting the light dissipate, I gasp for breath. The struggle to perform easy earth magic, something that was done in the blink of an eye before I left Morbank, brings a tear to my eye. I can't believe

I just stopped. Something that was as essential to me as breathing became nonexistent.

A shiver runs down my spine—the spell used to keep us away, an insidious intrusion—and I thank the goddess that it was discovered and we can now fight back.

Having recovered my breath, I send out another gentle pulse of seeking magic and feel all the plump, juicy kernels under the ground, just waiting for the right combination of elements to burst to life. I release the spell, and a wave of exhaustion flows through my body and mind. Turning, I walk back into the manor, happy with the night's work. I will continue this little exercise tomorrow after I get some much needed rest. I can't believe I only arrived back on the island today and how much has happened since I got here.

When I reach my room, the feeling of accomplishment joins the exhaustion, bringing a smile to my face. A clap of thunder booms across the sky, startling me, followed closely by a flash of lightning. The storm has well and truly arrived. Changing into a pair of sleep shorts and a tank top, I climb into bed, and I think I'm asleep before my head hits the pillow.

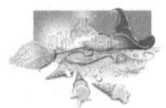

I'm up early the next morning. I'm going to head to the Buttered Biscuit, where Mom and I have an early breakfast meeting with Bram and Gerald to discuss renovations. Mom should be by to pick me up very soon, and I want to be downstairs waiting for her so she doesn't have to get out of the car.

Walking toward the elevator, I hear a sound.

"Psst!"

I look around, searching for the source of the noise.

"Tats! Over here."

The whisper is coming from a room just past the elevator. I walk over to it, and a hand reaches out and pulls me into the room before closing the door behind me.

"God, Ruby!" I shout, seeing who it is. "You scared the shit out of me. What are you doing here so early?"

Seeing a movement out of the corner of my eye, I turn and see Regan standing next to the window, watching me with a frown on his face.

"Oh, hey, Regan."

He nods at me, but the glare doesn't move.

Turning back to Ruby, I raise a brow. "Well?"

A sheepish look crosses her face. "Ah, we might have a small problem," she says, holding up her fingers to show how small a problem.

"We? I don't think so. What did you do?" I demand, my hands on my hips.

She goes to answer when Regan wanders out of the bathroom. Turning slowly, I look from the Regan that walked out of the bathroom to the one standing by the window.

My heart skips a beat. Looking between the two Regans, I turn quickly back to her. "What the fuck did you do?" I growl.

"Remember when I mentioned something about the replicating spell in that old book of Nana's? I went home and reread it, then made use of the blood from the napkin last night, and ta-da!" she exclaims like a game show host gesturing to the two Regans.

They are now standing next to each other. I circle them, examining them from head to toe. The frowning one is in a three-piece suit with his hair nicely brushed, and he has an uptight, tense look to him. The other one is dressed in jeans and a T-shirt, his hair is messy, and he is grinning at me. When I meet his eyes, he winks and says, "Hey, babe."

I struggle to keep the smile off my face.

"I specified aspects of Regan's personality to take care of certain things while he's gone. This one" — she gestures to Uptight Regan— "can run the manor while he's gone, and this one can help with the inter-views." She gestures to Flirty Regan. "But I'm afraid something went wrong. They were both supposed to be efficient and goal oriented. This is Dudebro Regan before he met Susan." She gestures to the flirty one who keeps shooting heated looks in my direction. "He's a fucking man-whore," she mumbles in disgust.

A snort escapes my nose before I can help it. He blows a kiss in my direction, and I collapse into a heap of giggles on the floor. "Oh my god, Ruby. You have done some shit in the past, but this takes the cake. He's going to kill you," I tell her around the escaping giggles.

She joins me on the floor, a disgruntled look on her face. "I'm not sure what went wrong. I can't undo it either," she whines. "The spell runs for a set time, and I set it for a week."

More laughter escapes, and I hold my side, the laughter causing a stitch to form. "Oh my god! What are you going to do?"

She just shrugs as I struggle to get control of my laughter.

Looking between the two replicas, I shake my head at her. "You're just going to have to keep them out of the way." I push myself off the ground and stand up. "I have to go. Mom will be waiting for me. I think you should probably tell the original Regan what you've done."

She pales a little at this comment. "I was going to hide them until you left for the realms tomorrow," she says quietly, "and not tell anyone."

"Seriously?" I ask incredulously. "How did you think that was going to work? Sometimes, Ruby, your ideas get ahead of your own intelligence. Sort it out," I tell her firmly before leaving the room. The look of shame on her face as I leave makes me feel guilty, but I steel my spine and keep going.

Finally making it to the lobby, I step out of the elevator and walk across the foyer to the doors.

"Tatiana."

I hear my name called and turn around to see Regan standing behind the front desk. Shit!

Rubbing my eyes and grabbing the back of my neck to ward off the brewing tension headache, I walk back to the real Regan. Damn, he looks good. He's wearing jeans with a suit jacket. The green button-up shirt looks amazing against his reddish-brown hair, and his green eyes are sparkling with excitement.

Hoping my face shows none of my worries, I give him a smile. "Morning! How are you?" My phone message sound plays in my back pocket. Mom must be here.

"Good, thanks. I just wanted to let you know I've scheduled our realm jump for tomorrow morning. Meet me in the portal room at eight if you don't mind," he tells me while stacking some papers in his hands. "Don't forget to pack a bag for a couple of days."

"Great, thanks for letting me know, I'll be there. I've got to go, Mom's waiting," I say and hurry toward the exit. I don't want to get stuck talking to him and for him to figure out something is wrong.

Mom's little compact car is sitting in the circle driveway. I climb in and give her a kiss on the cheek.

"Morning, thanks for picking me up. Not being able to teleport is a pain. I'll need to get myself a car. Maybe a trip to Kingston is needed," I remark as she navigates around the circle. I cast my eye over the expanse that I planted last night, sending out a small wave of magic and feeling that all of my kernels survived and are ready for the next boost this evening.

Mom gives me a worried look. "Did you do some magic last night? I can feel your signature. How are you feeling?"

"Yes, I started on the cornfield. I was exhausted afterward, but in a good way. It feels good being able to do magic again."

The worry leaves her face, and she sighs in relief. "Thank goodness. So breakfast meeting, and then what are your plans for today?"

"Regan just told me we are going into the realms tomorrow, so I think I'll work on some recipes for some new flavors. Then we can get together when I get back, and I'll show you what I've been able to find in the realms and we can finalize the changes."

The concern on her face returns as we arrive at the Buttered Biscuit, and she stops the car. She puts her hand on my arm. "Oh, baby, I worry about you going into the realms underpowered. I know Regan is a powerful warlock in his own right, but I really wish your magic was back up to strength."

I pat her hand. "Mom, we'll be fine. We can't put it off until my magic has fully returned. The island needs these tours," I reassure her. "Come on, let's get some breakfast. You'll feel better after some good food."

CHAPTER
Seven

Regan

Watching Tatiana hurry out the door momentarily distracts me from my task. Her ass looks spectacular in those jeans, but a voice from the back room draws my focus.

"I'm sorry, Julie, what did you say?" I ask, turning to see Julie standing in the doorway to the back room, a frown on her face. Her hair is pulled into some tight updo, and her uniform is bordering on obscene with her breasts pushed up so far and the tight fabric accentuating everything she has to offer—nothing like the subtle elegance displayed by Tatiana, even in jeans and a shirt.

"Who is that woman? She was at dinner with you last night."

"That one?" I ask, pointing in the direction

Tatiana had just gone, and she nods, putting her hands on her hips. "I've never seen her before."

"That's Tatiana, Maddock's sister. She just moved back to town to refurbish the ice-cream store. She's staying here in exchange for helping with the haunted house and the maze we are going to run for Halloween."

A pout crosses her face, and the inner me rolls his eyes.

"I could have helped with that," she complains.

"You could have, you're right, but your rehire is temporary," I remind her gently. I'm not that much of an asshole. "If you want a permanent position, you're going to have to interview like all the others who have applied."

She huffs and crosses her arms. "Well, how do I get an interview?"

"Ruby is in charge of those. I'll let her know to add you to the list. She will be conducting them for the next couple of days."

Her frown deepens, but then her expression clears, and she smiles. "Thanks, Regan. I do love working here with you."

"Okay, now I need to head down to the portal and check on it." I turn and head toward the elevator. I can hear her heels on the floor behind me as she follows.

"Can I come with you? I've always wanted to see the portal," she pleads.

"Nope, you know the rules. No outsiders are allowed in the portal room. This is going to change with the tours, but they will still require a full back-ground and magic check. Remember, every person who comes through from the other realms is fully vetted before being allowed through. Each realm has a portal keeper, like we do, to enforce the rules."

I press the button to call the elevator and turn to face her.

"If you are successful with your interview and background check, I'll take you in with one of the tours if you want. I will need group leaders to do the tours, since I can't do them all myself and the council has insisted that they are escorted by a supernatural from this side. Someone needs to be held responsible for the safety and well-being of everyone involved."

She looks like she's swallowed something sour before, again, flashing me a smile. "That would be awesome."

I step into the elevator, putting my hand on the palm scanner to access the portal level. A sharp spike punches a tiny hole in my palm, and a drop of blood flows onto the biometric scanner. The door closes, and I'm pretty sure I don't imagine the look of fury that crosses her face.

I'm certain that's her worst nightmare of a job. She's too selfish to be responsible for the well-being and safety of others. I wonder if she will still apply for a position now.

The elevator comes to a stop, and the door opens to the portal embarking chamber. There are couches littered around the room for the comfort of the people traveling. The portal can only be locked onto one realm at a time, so this area is for those who are waiting for a different one.

The portal itself is nonoperational due to power fluctuations that have never happened before. Though the coven always has someone posted here, there is a rotation of four individuals to cover all shifts.

Walking across the waiting room, I enter the operations room off to the side. There is a huge window sitting in front of a control desk, and sitting behind the desk is William. William is my ex-wife's brother and not my favorite person. He never has been, but his father's family has been a member of the coven for generations, and just because his sister was untrustworthy doesn't mean he is—though he does give off a slightly slimy vibe. Neither of my children will spend time with him. Not that he has shown any interest in getting to know them.

He doesn't hear me enter the room because he has a set of headphones on over his greasy, stringy hair, and from the smell in the space, I can tell he hasn't showered recently either. He's so focused entirely on the screen in front of him, he hasn't even noticed me walk past the window. He taps away furiously on the computer keyboard. It's actually amazing—the computer, not that he can type. It's linked with all the realms and allows messages to be sent back and forth requesting passage because Earth is the only inter-connecting realm for all the others. It's the waypoint between all other realms.

Say you want to go from the fae to the shifter

realm. You have to go through Earth. There is no other choice. There are many realms, but the fae, shifter, and vampire realms are the ones that request the most passage. I guess they can easily pass for human, so visiting Earth has always been an option. Angels have no interest in interacting with humans, though they must have once upon a time due to the religious stories. It's the same with the demons, and although there are higher demons who can take human form, most are weird creatures who would scare the pants off the average person.

I clear my throat loudly to get his attention, and he almost falls off his chair in fright. He blanks the screen and turns to face me. "Fuck, man, I didn't hear you. What's up?"

"Just letting you know we need the portal operational tomorrow," I tell him. "The fae realm at eight, please." I walk over to the schedule pinned on the wall. "Who's on the morning shift for the next couple of days?" I run my finger down the names until I get to the right section. "Okay, it's Mac. I'll give him a rundown on my timeline for visits and let him fill you all in."

"Is this to finalize the realm tours? I guess it's going to be busy over the next couple of days, huh?" William asks, curiosity evident in his voice.

"Not over the next couple of days, but by Halloween, hopefully," I reply. "We will limit travel for a couple more days and slowly increase the time allowed again. Hopefully, the power fluctuations will even out."

"Ah, yeah, of course, no problem. Whatever you say, you're the boss," he says, swallowing nervously. This is precisely what I meant about being slimy. He is nervous all the time, and it drives me nuts. Man up.

"Okay, well, good talk." Waving, I leave the operations room and head back to the elevator.

When it arrives back in reception, the doors open, and I'm greeted by a gross sight. Ruby's damn cat Sugar is sitting directly in front of the elevator, licking her butt like there will be no tomorrow.

My nose wrinkles. "Damn it, Sugar, has Ruby still not wormed you? You can't sit in the foyer of the manor and lick your ass."

Picking her up, I shove her under my arm and march to the doors but stop when I hear Julie call my name. She rushes over to me, and as she gets to me, Sugar hisses at her and leaps from my arms, taking a swipe at her.

"Shit!" I manage to avoid the claws, but Julie is not quite so lucky, and Sugar gets her on the hand.

Screeching, she aims a kick at Sugar, who has landed at our feet.

Before she can connect, I bend down and pick her up by the scruff of her neck and march her to the doors. "Go on, out with you. And do that butt licking in private." Giving her a quick scratch behind the ears, I shove her outside.

Taking a deep breath, I turn around to face Julie's wrath. My eyes focus on her hand, noting Sugar has done an excellent job. Three deep scratches are welling with drops of blood, and there is a look of murder in her eyes as she stares through the doors at Sugar, who is pacing back and forth in front of the manor doors like a sentry on watch.

Sighing, I take her by the arm. "Come on, let's get that cleaned up." We walk back to the reception desk and enter the office behind it. I sit Julie down on a chair. "I can either perform a spell or get you a Band-Aid. Your choice," I tell her, giving her two options. I don't want to assume a spell is okay and then for her to freak out if it's not.

A nervous look crosses her face. "Oh, ah, no, a Band-Aid will be fine, please."

Nodding my head, I rummage around in the cupboard for a first aid kit. "What was it that you were rushing over to tell me?" I ask, pulling a bit of gauze out of the kit and gently dabbing at the scratches.

"Oh, I just checked a man in while you were downstairs," she tells me, watching me dab at the scratches before looking up at me. "No booking, but a walk-in. He's visiting friends on the island and was supposed to be staying in town with them, but their spare bedroom flooded or something."

"Really? That's great. You did warn him about the lack of staff at the moment, though, didn't you?" I ask her quickly, putting some antiseptic on her wound. The last thing I need is complaints while I'm gone.

She nods as I finish off with a Band-Aid over her

scratches. "Yes, seems like a nice guy. Had an accent, but he was very charming."

"Excellent. There you go, you are all done. I'm going to head back upstairs to my office now and go through the applications for realm tours and start the background checks. Let me know if you need anything."

She flutters her eyelashes at me and puts her hand on mine. "Thank you so much for fixing my hand, Regan." The smile drops. "That cat is a menace and should be put down. Every time I see it, it's licking its ass. It must have something wrong with it."

Another sigh leaves my mouth. "To be honest, Julie, I've never seen Sugar attack anyone like that. The kids adore her, and she's usually friendly to everyone. I'll talk to Ruby about her. Maybe she's not well."

Leaving the office, I head around the reception desk and back to the elevator. I glance at my watch and notice it's not even half-past nine. I rub a hand over my weary eyes. I seriously need a day off and some decent sleep.

As I'm about to hit the call button, the elevator opens in front of me, and a body barrels out in a hurry, knocking me, and it, off balance.

Putting up my hands, I steady us both before looking at the person. "Ruby? What the hell are you doing here this morning, and why are you in such a hurry?"

"Shit, I'm late to open the candy store, and of

course I can't teleport from upstairs." The words tumble out of her mouth.

"But what were you doing upstairs? Were you looking for me?"

She glances around the foyer as if looking for a reason. "Ah, no. Look, Regan, don't go into Room 119. I um…" She trails off, looking guilty.

I hold up my hands, stopping her. "Look, I don't want to know. I don't need the details about anything that has to do with you and Maddock."

A bright smile covers her face. "Yes, that's it. Sex surprise for Maddock. Don't go in there."

Covering my ears, I shout, "Nope, don't want to know! Did you make sure the room shows as unavailable on the computer?" She nods her head. "Well, that's fine, though why you have to use one of my hotel rooms when you have a perfectly good cottage of your own is beyond me."

"Roleplay," she calls as she heads away from the elevator. "I'm the turndown service." She turns and winks at me, and with a snap of her fingers, she disappears.

I shake my head and grab the bridge of my nose, squeezing in the hope to ward off the headache that is brewing, before stepping into the elevator. "Gross. I really didn't need to know that," I mutter.

I spend the day doing background checks and finalizing the first tour group. I will send out the invitations when we return from the realms. When that's done, I go through the applications Ruby organized interviews for, impressed with the people who have applied, and also do their background checks so we can offer them positions straight away without having to wait. Having magical means to do the checks makes the process so much quicker.

Finishing up, I teleport to my parents' place for dinner and to kiss the twins goodnight. They are staying there tonight so tomorrow morning isn't such a rush. I was going to head to the Hamster for a drink, but I'm too damn tired, so I head back to the manor. Setting my alarm on my phone, I'm out before my head even hits the pillow.

CHAPTER
Eight

Tatiana.

After my breakfast meeting, I sit in the ice-cream shop with my laptop and finalize the plans for the store. Mom and I spend the day writing recipes and brainstorming ideas about flavor combinations.

Before we know it, we are going to have more than that brand that boasts about having more than thirty-one flavors. Once we have the recipes nailed down, Mom decides to clean out the freezer, which is being replaced. We put a sign up in the window advertising free ice cream while stock lasts. Mom also sends a message over to the local elementary school.

All afternoon, we are inundated by families clamoring for free ice cream. Dad and Maddock are called in from the blacksmiths, and between the four of us, we manage.

Finally, we run out of supplies, and we wave goodbye to the last few customers as they stumble out the door. By now, every person on this island has had at least one ice-cream cone, if not a couple.

Mom collapses into a booth, a massive breath of air escaping her mouth. "Well, that was something. I'm exhausted."

Maddock pulls her up out of the booth, takes the tea towel out of Dad's hand, and steers them both toward the door. "Go, we've got this," he tells them.

Mom tears up, a grateful look crossing her features. "Are you sure?" she asks, looking at me.

"Consider this a trial run for retirement," I assure her. "Go have dinner at the Hamster or go home and have some time together." I wink, and she blushes, while Dad quickly puts his hand on her back and hurries her out the door without a backward glance.

I head to the kitchen, and the sight has me groaning and slumping against the doorframe. The mound of dirty ice cream tubs is enormous.

Maddock pushes past me and laughs. "Tatiana, you are still thinking like a human." He snaps his fingers, and the dirty tubs are instantly stacked and soapy water is in the sink.

He throws me a tea towel, and I snatch it out of the air before it hits the ground. "What the hell? Why didn't you just clean them all?" I grumble at him.

He starts washing the tubs and passing them to me. "Well, maybe I want to chat with my baby sister."

"Pfft, baby sister. I'm ten months younger, we're the same age," I complain while shaking the suds off the tub before drying it.

"Yes, but you are younger. I just want to hear about your life. I've missed you over the last couple of years. Every time I tried to call you, your phone went to voicemail. If I called your home phone, Marco would answer, and he obviously wasn't passing on the messages," he mutters.

"Actually, he was. He wasn't a complete asshole, but it was like he was telling me someone random was calling. It didn't register to me that it was family and I should call them back."

"Not a complete asshole? Wasn't he anti-supe? What were you thinking?" His questions make me pause.

"Kind of. He came from a strict Catholic family. Even with the proof of the paranormal and other realms, they believe being supernatural is against God's law or something like that. I don't know, I think it was just an excuse to be assholes. But Marco wasn't as bad as his parents. He was more tolerant, I guess. Not as judgmental. I thought he was the one. I was willing to give up my magic for him..." I trail off.

Maddock stops what he is doing and looks at me incredulously. "Are you fucking kidding me?"

I look down at the floor in shame and shrug my shoulders. "Yeah! You've got to understand it was like living in an alternate reality. I didn't think about it. It was like you guys, and magic, didn't even factor into my life. It wasn't until Ruby turned up at the ice-cream store that everything came back into focus. It was like the fog finally lifted, and I realized how much I had neglected my real life. I was so worried that you guys wouldn't forgive me."

I place my hand on my stomach, remembering the sick feeling that came over me when Ruby told me everything.

"I was going to get Marco to take some time off and come back with me for a while, but that obviously changed the minute I got back to our home. To be honest, now that I look back, he never questioned me about where I came from or about my family in general. Who knows, maybe it was part of the spell, or maybe he really didn't care." I shrug my shoulders and grab another tub to dry. "It doesn't matter now. That part of my life is done, and I really am happy to be home."

He nudges me with his hip but keeps washing the tubs. "And we're happy to have you home. Except now you're leaving again. You make sure you are careful in the realms. Remember, nobody is inherently good or bad. There are shades of gray everywhere."

Rolling my eyes at the big brother act, I assure him I will be fine. "Look, all I'm doing is attending some meetings with Regan. Galan has arranged for his sister to accompany me to the main fae market. I'm not actually sure what the vampire or shifter realms will have to offer in the way of ingredients, so I'm not expecting too much. The fae realm was the main goal."

He nods and steps back from the sink, snapping his fingers, and the huge pile disappears before reappearing on the shelves sparkling clean and stacked neatly. "All right then, good talk." He grabs the tea towel from my hand and dries his hands. "Hey, if you see Ruby at the manor when you get back there, can you tell her that I've been trying to get in touch with her all day?"

Spinning quickly so he can't see my face, I walk back out to the front of the store. "Oh, yep, will do. I saw her this morning, and she had some plans to go hard on the candy making today because she has interviews over the next few days and won't have time to make more." *Damn you, Ruby, you owe me for lying for you.*

"Oh, yeah, that makes sense. Smart idea. Just have her call me, will you? Why don't you take off and I'll finish up here?" he suggests, and I don't wait for him to say anything else.

I'm heading toward the door before I remember that Mom drove me. "Crap, I don't have a car."

"Heads-up!" Maddock's voice has me turning just in time to catch a set of keys. "Use my truck for now until you can get a car of your own, or your magic gets up to strength again."

My big brother is such a sweetheart. "Are you sure?" I ask him.

"Yeah, I'll just teleport, but I want you working on your magic."

I salute him with the keys in my hand. "Yes, sir. That's what I'm going to do now. The cornfield needs another nudge, then I need to pack a bag for tomorrow." Smacking a kiss on his cheek, I hurry out the front door, the chimes ringing out into the cold evening air as it closes behind me.

Whoa, the temperature has really dropped. The sky is filled with thick, black clouds, and the smell of snow is in the air. It won't be long before Morbank is covered with a blanket of white.

Rubbing my hands against my arms, I run to Maddock's truck, throw open the door, and climb in. Cranking the engine, I turn the heat up to full blast and let the truck idle until it starts to put out some heat, then I shift it into gear and head to the manor.

After parking Maddock's truck in the designated area, I rush upstairs to grab a jacket from my room. It's too cold for me to stand out in the open without it. I'll need to get some warmer clothes as well now that I am back home.

As I walk toward the elevator, I see a door to a cleaning closet is open, and there's a shuffling sound coming from inside. That's strange, there shouldn't be any housekeepers working this evening. Regan told me they do all their rounds in the morning.

Creeping forward, I put my hand up to the doorway to open it but stop. Am I really going to do this? That move kills someone every time in every B-grade horror flick Ruby has made me sit through. My heart starts to pound, and my breath hitches.

Something clatters like it's been dropped, making me jump, and a small yelp leaves my mouth. I hear a male's voice swearing. That sounds like Regan. Letting go of the fear, I open the door wide. The closet is dark, but the light from the corridor illuminates the inside. Regan drops what he is picking up and grabs hold of my arm, pulling me into the closet and shutting the door behind us.

It's pitch black, and the sharp smell of cleaning chemicals fills the air, but before I can say anything, his mouth is on mine. He plunges his tongue into my mouth while shoving me against the closet door. His hands roam my body like he's a blind man searching for a way out. He grinds his erection against my jean-clad pussy, dragging a moan from me. He pulls his mouth away from mine and whispers in my ear.

"How about you get on your knees and suck my cock for me like a good girl?"

I freeze. *What did he just say?*

"Come on, babe, suck my cock, and I'll give you the ride of your life." Although the dirty talk is setting my panties on fire, this is not my Regan. Lifting my knee, I launch it into his crotch, and as he doubles over in pain, I shove him away from the door and storm out.

"Oh my god, Tatiana." Ruby's voice has a hint of panic in it as I turn to face her with my hands on my hips. "Something happened." She rushes toward me from the direction of Room 119.

"Hmm, I would say so," I reply, tapping my foot in annoyance, and I point toward the closet.

"Oh! Which one?" she asks quietly.

"Well, from his dirty mouth, I would say it's probably Dudebro Regan." Who would have thought Regan would have that in him? Thank goodness I have a jacket on and Ruby can't see my nipples trying to escape.

Dudebro Regan stumbles out of the closet holding his crotch. "What did you go and do that for?" he whines.

Before he can say anything else, Ruby points her finger at him. "Immobilis!" she shouts, and Regan freezes like she pressed pause. She waves her finger at him, his body moves horizontally, and then she floats him back toward the room they were in this morning with me following behind.

"I'm so sorry, Tatiana. I turned my back to finally answer a text from Maddock, and one of them hit me over the head." Now that I look closely, she has a little lump on her forehead.

"Are you okay? Do you need to see a doctor?" I grab her to get a closer look. My concern overrides my annoyance, but she pulls away and shakes her head gingerly.

"No. I will just put this one back in his room, and then I have to search for the other one."

"Well, good luck. I'm going to go grow some corn. If I see him, I'll call you, and for goodness' sake, call Maddock. He's worried, but luckily he has been busy at the ice-cream store all afternoon."

She nods her head and floats Dudebro Regan into the room.

I continue on to the elevator and press the button. When it arrives, the doors open, and standing there, wrapped around each other, are Regan and Julie. Her hands are winding through his hair, and she has one leg wrapped around his hip. His hands are on her ass, and he has a leg between hers, allowing her to grind against it. His suit looks a little disheveled. Breaking the kiss, he turns to look at me. His mouth is smeared with red lipstick, and he has a slightly dazed and confused expression on his face.

I turn and call, "Ah, Ruby... I think I've found your other problem."

Her head pops out of the room, and she catches sight of the elevator's occupants. She rolls her eyes and mutters under her breath. "Fuck, I am going to get it when he finds out."

A snort escapes my mouth as I watch her storm toward the lift, grab Uptight Regan by the hand, and drag him back to the room before slamming the door behind her.

"Hey!" Julie complains, looking from the slammed door to me.

I just shrug my shoulders and enter the elevator. "Work stuff," I mumble, pushing the button for reception.

When it gets there, she flounces out of the lift and heads toward the exit. I walk slowly behind her, not wanting to get cornered and questioned. Before I can exit, Sugar, Ruby's cat, walks up and winds her way around my legs in greeting. Bending down, I stroke her soft fur and whisper some sweet nothings in her ear, then I head outside with her at my feet.

The sun has gone down, and Julie has disappeared. I wonder where she got off to so quickly. Maybe she had a car waiting. Dismissing her, I shove my hands deep into my pockets and cross the drive, heading toward my field. The moon is low on the horizon this evening, and the wind has picked up. A shiver flows down my spine, and I speed up. The quicker I can get this done, the faster I can go back inside.

Taking a deep breath, I slowly send out another pulse of magic. This one is slightly bigger than last night's. Again, it flows out over the field, sending a signal to the little sprouts to grow. It's like watching a time-lapse video. The whole field wriggles like it's covered in worms, and the green tips of the stalks poke their way out of the ground. Holding the magic, I coax them to grow until they are about three inches tall, gritting my teeth against the pressure. Finally, with a gasp, I let the magic flow from me, releasing it to the atmosphere. I'm certainly not cold now, the strain from holding the magic bringing a bead of sweat to my brow.

I crouch down and run my hand over a patch close to me. Happy with the result, I turn and head inside. Deciding I probably need to start doing more magic, I open the door to the manor with a dramatic wave of my hand and giggle from the joy of it. I missed this.

Once back inside, I press the button for the elevator, ready to get warm, when something stops me. I can feel a residual buzz of magic. It's not mine, but when I look around, I don't see anyone else. That's strange, where is it coming from? As quickly as it started, it stops. It's like it never happened. Maybe I imagined it. Shaking my head, I go inside.

When I get back upstairs, I head straight into the bathroom and have a quick shower to wash off the grime from the day. Dressing in a tank top and short shorts, I sit down on the couch and pull out my laptop to do some haunted house research.

Sitting open on the coffee table in front of me is my notebook with all the notes I took from Galan and the recipes Mom and I came up with today. That's odd. I look around the room. My handbag is where I left it when I came and got my jacket, and I could have sworn I left the notebook in there.

Maybe Ruby came back to tell me something while I was downstairs. I wouldn't put it past her to snoop—the girl has no boundaries.

Shaking off the uneasy feeling, I spend the next couple of hours ordering decorations for the haunted house and making plans. Next, I throw a change of clothes into a backpack and add my notebook on top. There's no point in taking my phone into the realms since there will be no reception, and the laptop is too bulky for me to carry around for a short trip.

When I'm packed, I set my alarm and climb into bed, happy with what I achieved for the day.

Sleep is a long time coming. The excitement for

tomorrow has butterflies in my tummy buzzing. My thoughts then turn to Dudebro Regan's dirty words and actions, and that ignites a different kind of feeling lower than my stomach. Eventually, with some deep breathing exercises, I'm able to shut off and get a couple hours of sleep.

CHAPTER
Nine

Tatiana

My alarm has me jumping out of bed quicker than I have in years. Throwing on a pair of cargo pants and a shirt, I sit down on the bed and pull on my hiking boots. I didn't think to ask Regan if the dress code was casual or fancy. Oh well, not much I can do now.

Grabbing my backpack, I head out to have a quick breakfast before we leave, but when I open the door to my room, I come to a dead halt. Sitting in front of my door is a bloody, dead rat. What the hell? Before I can do anything, Regan's door opens across the hall, and he walks out with damp hair, but he's dressed similarly to me. Phew, I breathe a sigh of relief.

"Oh, hey, good timing," he says as he pulls his door closed and steps farther into the corridor before stopping and noticing what I'm looking at.

"Fuck. Sugar must have brought you a present last night."

"Up an elevator?" We both turn to look at the elevator and then back toward the rat. "She's one clever cat, but does she usually make such a mess?" Bending down, I look at the rat's body. It looks like it had its throat torn out. "She's a bit of a messy eater."

"She's a strange one. Maybe she snuck in when someone was using the elevator. We do have a couple of guests. Come on, let's have some breakfast, and I'll have housekeeping deal with it."

"No, it's okay, I've got this," I tell him. Concentrating on the rat, I snap my fingers and it disappears, bloodstain and all. No trace of the mess is left behind, and there's no sign of any weariness for me. I smile brightly at Regan. "That's getting so much easier. It feels so good to use it again."

He slings an arm around my shoulders and propels me toward the elevator before dropping it again. "I'm glad. I can't imagine what it would be like not to have my magic."

I frown. "I was telling Maddock last night that I didn't even notice. It was like I had forgotten I had it."

He goes to say something, but there is a thumping sound against the door for Room 119 as we walk past it. Regan rubs the back of his neck, like he's developing a headache, and the door cracks open before Ruby eases her way out.

"Oh, hey, hi, guys."

"Bloody hell, Ruby. Those rooms are supposed to

be soundproof. What the fuck are you doing that we could hear it out here?" he growls at his sister, and she looks at the ground, embarrassed.

I keep my amusement to myself. I don't want him to grill me for details.

A bruise shaped like a handprint is blossoming around her neck, and when Regan spots it, he flips his shit. He rushes toward Ruby and shakes her. "What the fuck is he doing to you? I'll kill him!"

She shoots me a desperate look for help, and I step forward. "Ah, Regan… Are you really sure you want to know what they are doing? Ruby doesn't seem to be upset. She just looks a little flushed."

He looks at her and raises an eyebrow, and she quickly shakes her head.

I grab Regan by the arm and guide him away. "What a couple does in the bedroom is none of our business as long as it's consensual."

He turns to look back at Ruby.

"Oh, it is. Trust me, it is. I'm giving as good as I'm getting."

Regan turns a little green at this and keeps walking, muttering under his breath.

I rush quickly back to Ruby, grabbing her arm. "Are you really okay? Tell Maddock what's going on. It looks and sounds like you are going to need help controlling them," I say, nodding to the bruise.

"Uptight Regan is fine and understands his role in what is going on, but Dudebro Regan is a handful. He wants out and isn't afraid to try and get it," she whispers.

I shake my head and run to catch up with Regan. He's still muttering under his breath as we enter the elevator and head down to the restaurant.

"Regan, stop, they are two consenting adults. Let it go." I feel horrible lying to him, but I don't want to keep talking about it, and I certainly don't want to tell him the truth because he may decide not to go.

We have a quiet breakfast in the restaurant. Pru pops her head out of the kitchen and wishes us luck. She's the chef for the manor today, and she tells me she can't wait until Ruby does her interviews. She has a few scheduled, but the chef ones are tomorrow, and of course Regan will need to meet all of the potentials and do the final sign off when we come back.

Finally, we head down to the portal room. A buzz of excitement flows through my body. I've never been through the portal before, not many people have from this side, but that's all about to change now.

We head to the office to speak to the portal operator. Mac is an older member of our coven of my mom and dad's generation, and he is a friendly jovial type. He used to play Santa Claus at the coven Christmas parties when we were kids. Judging by his belly, he may still be doing it.

"Tatiana, love, good to see you back." He gives me a hug and steps back, holding me at arm's length. "Oh, and aren't you a pretty one? Don't you think, Regan? I should introduce you to my nephew." He winks at me as Regan answers him.

"She certainly has grown up," he mutters

noncommittally, and I shoot him a death look. He blushes but doesn't say anything else.

Okay then.

"Mac, like I discussed with you yesterday on the phone, we're going to the fae realm today. We've been invited to stay overnight with Galan's family, and then if you could open the portal again tomorrow morning at ten, we'll head to the vampire realm where we'll stay with Cole, and then onto the shifter realm on the last day. But we won't stay overnight there. We will be home in the evening."

"Sure thing, Regan. I've written it all down and set the coordinates and times into the computer already. Even if I'm not here and whoever is on forgets, the portal will still go."

"Really?" I ask in surprise.

Mac nods his head. "Yeah, it's a backup thing, and only I have the code to do it. The portal is manned twenty-four seven, so we don't use it very often."

"Alright, let's go," Regan says to me, and we head back out into the portal room.

The portal is a huge doorway shaped piece of wood with runes carved into it. It's wide enough and high enough to drive a truck through and sits at one end of the room with the waiting area in front of it.

We stand in front of it, and there's a slight tingling in the air as goosebumps erupt on my arms. I give them a quick rub, and Regan smiles, looking at my arms.

"That used to happen to me the first couple of times too, but I'm used to it now."

Suddenly, a cloudy mist appears within the frame. The residual magic feels similar to the one I felt last night, but it can't be because this is the first time the portal has been operational in a while. Frowning, I start to say something to Regan, but he doesn't give me a chance.

"Come on." He grabs my hand, and we walk together through the mist.

It feels just like walking through actual mist, leaving a damp feeling on my skin. It's cold, and my breath comes out in puffs, the air chilling my throat as I breathe in and out.

We walk about ten steps, then the mist clears, and we appear on the far side of the portal. My mouth drops open in shock, and Regan laughs at my reaction.

"I was exactly the same when I first came here. It's a highly guarded secret that the fae love shocking visitors with. There is some sort of geas put on you when you leave that doesn't allow you to talk about what you see. You can speak about general stuff, like you had a good time, but if someone asks you to describe it specifically, you end up choking on your words."

The portal is on top of a tall building that is the highest point of a futuristic-looking city. Whatever material the buildings are made of is reflective, and they glimmer like diamonds, all shiny and sparkly. It's quite blinding.

Shading my eyes, I turn in a full circle. The city is circular in shape, and on its edges is a forest that stretches as far as the eye can see. The trees are humongous, with crazy colored leaves. There is a lot of green, but I can see trees in shades of purple, blue, and pink too. The air is humid and warm, a far cry from the miserable, stormy weather of Morbank Island. The sky shimmers with vapors of green, gold, and purple, like Earth's Aurora Borealis, lending a weird sparkle to the landscape. It's quite magical.

A noise off to the side catches my attention, and I turn to see what it is. Regan is talking to a man and a woman. Both are tall and elegant with dark hair. The man wears his long and has a gold circlet wrapped around his head, while the woman's hair hangs in two braids over her shoulders with silver ribbons wrapped through it. Both are wearing silver clothes, and when they turn to look at me, I realize that their eyes are bright emerald green.

Regan gestures to me, and I walk over to the group. "This is Crown Prince Aven Silvershadow and Princess Tempest Silvershadow. They are Galan's brother and sister. This is Tatiana Crane."

I gape in shock, and the crown prince laughs as he grips my hand and places a kiss on the back of it.

"Ah, I see by your reaction you didn't know our dear brother is a prince. Well, he is only a spare, so it doesn't really matter," he sneers. "He was always happy slumming it in our family vineyard. Then he turned his back on us for the human realm." The way he says that makes it obvious he wouldn't spit on the human realm if it were on fire. What a dick.

Extracting my hand from his, I turn to the

woman. She smiles kindly, and her voice is like rain on a rooftop, soothing and gentle. "Welcome, Tatiana. Galan messaged me and asked me to escort you to the market."

"Thank you. I'm really looking forward to seeing what the market has to offer."

"Shall we leave the men to it and meet back up after lunchtime?" she suggests.

I look to Regan to check, and he nods his head. The siblings lead us to an elevator. The height of the building causes a nervous shudder to flow through my body. Ugh, I don't mind heights, but this is super high, and there are no railings.

"Whoa, that's high. An interesting place to put a portal," I babble, my nerves getting the better of me.

The crown prince's curled lip expresses his disdain at my comment. "It's a good security measure. Only one way in and out. And we can always push intruders off the side." The door closes, and he presses a button on the wall.

The intense feeling of the elevator moving makes my stomach lurch, but it's over so quickly that I stumble slightly. Aven strides off the elevator with Regan following swiftly behind him.

"Huh." I must say it out loud, because Tempest turns to me with a questioning look. "He's nothing like Galan, is he?" I gesture in the direction they went as the lift closes again.

She scoffs, and her demeanor changes completely. All the tension in her body disappears, and she takes a deep breath and lets it out before answering me.

"God, no! When we were kids, we were like the three musketeers. Being royalty is hard. We are always in the spotlight, people fawn over us, and we're never sure who our real friends are. So we stuck together. Eventually, though, Aven started to believe his own press, and all the ass-kissers got into his head, and he became an arrogant ass with an inflated sense of self-worth. It has gotten worse. My father is due to step down soon, and Aven will be taking his place as king."

She looks at me with surprise in her eyes and slaps a hand over her mouth.

"Shit. I shouldn't have said that. But you're the first person who hasn't groveled to me in ages." She sighs and shakes her head. "I miss Galan. I understand why he left. He found his true mate. God, I'm so envious, but he always knew how to deal with Aven."

The elevator comes to a stop, and she takes a deep breath and puts on the serene smile again before walking out and gesturing for me to follow. My eyes must be bugging out of my head as I look around the foyer of the big building. I feel like I have stepped into a futuristic sci-fi film.

Tempest laughs at me. "Not what you were expecting?" she asks.

My amazed mind can't comprehend what I'm seeing, so I shake my head. "No, I was expecting lots of nature and maybe a castle and a village and lots of animals." My mind was firmly set on what Disney has portrayed fairies as over the years.

"We do have all of that, but the capital city is a lot more modern, as you can see." She spreads her arms like a gameshow host before winking at me and leading me outside onto the sidewalk. What looks like a car pulls up next to us. It is hovering, with a pale pink light illuminating the surface of the road underneath.

"Hovercars?" I gasp and watch as she opens the back door and climbs in before moving over and making room for me. "Come on, Tatiana. The market is on the outskirts of town. If we hurry, we might be able to see some talking animals."

"Really?" I ask in amazement as I climb into the back seat of the hover limo.

Tempest can't keep a straight face any longer. "No, I'm just messing with you. The only animals that can talk are shifters, and they don't do it in their animal form." Her laughter is like a bell ringing.

I stick my tongue out at her and grumble, "Bitch," under my breath.

She starts to calm down. "Oh, that was so much fun. Galan told me how movies and TV portray fairies in your world. I've been dying to trick someone with that. Thank you."

"Glad I could help you out," I grumble again, and she reaches out and grabs my hand. "Oh, Tatiana, really, I am sorry. I think you and I are going to be great friends."

She releases my hand and leans back as the city flies past us at a rapid rate. My eyes are glued to the view out my window, but I have more questions. "I know the fae have similar magic to the witches, and that your gods and goddess were related to ours, but what makes the fae realm different from the human realm?"

"Hmm, yes, you have a race of non-magic people, humans, and your land is dormant, where we have many different species of fae, all with their own inherent magic, and the land itself is magical—even though the animals don't talk." She shoots me a wink. "They all have some form of magic. The bunnies you will see are nothing like the ones in the human realm, as they are carnivores as opposed to your herbivores. The magic of this realm has twisted everything slightly. If you find yourself unescorted in the fae realm, be very wary of all the animals around you, even if they look like something from Earth. Most things will bite or be venomous here." Her voice has turned grave with this warning. "But you don't need to worry about that today."

"Okay, I have one more question, and if you laugh, I will hex you with itchy crotch rash," I threaten her, and her laughter rings out again before she bites her lip in an attempt to keep a straight face.

"Okay, I'm ready. Go."

"Pretty fairies with wings about this big." I hold my thumb and finger apart a couple of inches. "Real or not?"

"They are real," she confirms, and my heart sings with joy.

"Yes, that's awesome." I fist-bump the air.

"But they are nasty little shits, and if they bite

you, the venom in their bite eats away at the skin with a flesh-eating bacteria."

I look at her closely to see if she's pulling my leg again, but her face is dead serious. "Well, fuck." I drop back against the seat in disappointment and ignore the outside as we continue onto the market. "Tempest, you do know you've destroyed all my childhood fantasies. Maybe we won't include any of that information in the guided tour."

Her tinkling laugh fills the car again.

Ten

Regan

After I leave Tatiana in Tempest's capable hands, I sit down with the king and his council to finalize the tour details. Everyone seems really pleased with the upcoming joint venture and furthering the relationships between the realms. King Florian confirms that the initial tour will be the first week in November and hands me over to his prime minister to nail down the details since he has other things to attend to. Out of the corner of my eye, I see Aven and his dour expression.

"Hang on, Father. What's in it for us?" His father frowns at him. "No, the witches are benefitting from this, but the fae get nothing out of it apart from 'good relations.' Don't glare at me. I would be a poor future ruler if I didn't think about my people." His tone is condescending, and I can see various aides around the table rolling their eyes, but everyone looks at me.

"The fae market is on the tour, so I would assume revenue for the vendors. Don't forget there are more opportunities for the fae to travel to our realm as well."

"Pff, why would the fae want to travel to a dirty realm like Earth?"

I look at King Florian, and he is scowling at his oldest child, but he doesn't step in.

"I guess if the tours work, then the opportunity to extend them to lengthy vacations or even relocation are options. Again, more revenue for the fae."

"Visas. I want every person to visit the fae realm to pay for a visa," he announces to the room. "That should be fair compensation to my people."

The council erupts into protests, and the annoyance I'm feeling surges into anger. "You forget that we operate the portal. It was gifted to us by our goddess, and we can easily cut the fae realm off."

The crown prince shoots me a look filled with venom and sneers, "Be very careful with your threats. You may find they are empty if we don't care that we are cut off."

I smile at him. "Are you sure you want the gateway to all the other realms permanently closed? How would your people feel then?"

The council members are shaking their heads and muttering.

The king leans closer to the prince, a furious look

on his face, but I can't hear what he is saying around the chatter.

The advisor to my left snorts under his breath. "Yeah, right, like the people will ever see any of it."

I raise a questioning eyebrow, but he shakes his head and clamps his lips shut, refusing to elaborate, but the prince is too busy arguing with the king to notice.

"Silence!" the king shouts. "There will be no visa to start with, and we will reassess the situation after the first couple of groups."

The crown prince has a smug look on his face as he leans back in his chair with his arms crossed.

The king closes the meeting, and everyone stands around the table as he and Aven leave the room, taking a lot of the tension with them. Everyone else starts to filter out except for the man who made the comment before. Now that I look closer, I recognize him as the king's brother-in-law and prime minister.

"So, tell me, Helio, what was that little comment you muttered under your breath earlier?"

He looks around the room to make sure no one is still within hearing distance. "The crown prince has become a real problem. He has an advisor who is whispering in his ear and sycophantic followers to cater to his every whim. The crown prince is also a fairy dust and vampire bite addict."

I turn to look at the prime minister wryly. "You mean he is a sex addict?"

He nods his head. "Yes, he hides it well, and I'm sure his advisor gave him some potion this morning to sober him up, but he is a nasty piece of work. He has started keeping a harem, and some of the women are possibly there against their will. I know for sure one of the vampire women is. He starves her until she's desperate because she refuses to bite him. Then, when she's starving and gives in and she bites him, he fucks his harem women at the same time. He wears a charm that prevents her from draining him or ripping his throat out."

"Damn, I knew he was an asshole, but not to this extent. Why doesn't the king do anything?"

"Neither he nor my sister have been able to do anything. They've tried to fire the advisor, but Aven won't hear of it. Unless someone can convince Galan to return home, he's our only option."

"That's ridiculous. Make Tempest queen instead," I suggest.

He rolls his eyes in annoyance. "She would make a wonderful queen, but fae law says it has to be passed down through the male line. We are quietly doing research into how to change that, but if that gets out, there might be some suspicious deaths, so keep that to yourself."

Quietly amused at the gossipy fae—no secrets in this realm—but also perturbed at the info he has given me, I assure him that I wouldn't speak a word of it.

We turn to the matter of the tours, setting up an itinerary of places to view. At this stage, each visit will be a day long, and the group will return to the manor each evening before departing for the next realm the following day. We choose the fae market, fairy village—though they will be required to drink a potion to limit the effects of fairy dust—and the mermaid pool. We also decide on the dragon nesting ground from a distance and the alicorn grazing field. Lunch will be a fae tavern run by a clurichaun—they are similar to a leprechaun, but known for their great love of drinking. His bar is usually a rowdy, fun affair that should please the tourists.

After thinking about Aven's behavior a little more, I ask Helio a question that has been bugging me. "Is the general population of the fae realm alright with this initiative? I don't want to start and have them attacked by hostile natives."

"Oh no," he reassures me. "The locals are excited and hope that it can eventually be a two-way thing. More and more fae are curious about the other realms, and travel has been strictly regulated up until now. They are hoping this will become a new market. Earth, as well as the vampire and shifter realms, are real draws."

"That's a relief." Some of the tension escapes my shoulders.

Lunch is brought to us, and we spend the afternoon going over possible details for turning the tours to longer stays. We also discuss fae law and the relevant information visitors will need to have if they are going to remain without someone responsible for them like a tour guide.

Meanwhile, At The Manor

Ruby

Maddock pulls at his dark hair in frustration as he takes in the view in front of him. "Ruby, what the ever-loving fuck did you do?" he growls in his rumbly voice that usually puckers my nipples, but this time I know I'm not going to get lucky, judging by the look on his face.

"Hey, don't talk to her like that." Dudebro Regan may be an ass, but he still recognizes me as his sister. I nod my thanks to him, and he puts his handcuffed fists out for a bump. I go to bump it, but Maddock pushes my hand down, and his scowl deepens.

"Explain! Now!"

Hmm, I like this side of him. Maybe I can remind him of it later. Oh, perhaps he's going to spank me. My mind drifts, and I squirm with the fantasy.

"Ruby!"

His shout brings me back, and I blow out a big sigh. Jesus, it seems all I've been doing the last few days is sighing. "I thought I was helping. I mentioned the replicating spell I found."

"Yeah, but I didn't think you would give it a try. You were going to call your nana first."

I wave my hand at him in frustration. "I tried, but she and Pop are on a cruise. I couldn't reach her."

He rolls his eyes. "Did you try scrying her?" I can feel the burn on my cheeks at his question, and he prompts, "Well?"

"Um, yes. She was busy. With Pop."

He blanches at the information and holds a hand up to stop me. "Forget I asked."

I watch as he paces back and forth in front of the two Regans. Dudebro is tied to a chair, his hands cuffed in front of him, but Uptight is sitting quietly on the bed watching us.

"Look, I only meant to replicate one," I tell him, pointing to Uptight. "He was supposed to sit quietly during the interviews and look all menacing and official. Plus, he can pick up some of the slack in the manor while Regan's gone. But I ended up with him and man-whore over there." I turn to him with my hands on my hips. "You went to college with him. How come this is the first I'm hearing about his man-whore ways? Were you like that too?"

A surprised look covers his face before he grimaces and tries to change the subject. "It doesn't matter now. What are you going to do?"

"Don't think I didn't notice you changed the subject. We will come back to this conversation," I promise him.

Sitting down on the bed next to Uptight, I snap my fingers, and a mug of coffee appears in my hand. Taking a sip, I relax slightly.

"Simple! We continue as planned. He will come

with us and do exactly what I say." I send a death glare at Uptight, and he just nods his head once. Shaking my head, I turn to Dudebro. "And we'll kill this one."

Both Maddock's and Dudebro's eyes bug out of their heads, and Dudebro starts to blubber, "No. No, please don't. I'll do anything."

"Relax," I tell him, looking to Maddock. "I mean, we could, since he technically doesn't exist, but I think if I did, I would lose this one too, because the spell ties them together. We'll just leave him here tied up and do our interviews. We will put the do not disturb sign up again and gag him."

Poor Maddock. His hair is sticking out in all directions, and his body slumps in a defeated pose. I wonder what got to him the most—my spell or Nana having sex. Cue evil laugh. Setting my mug of coffee on the side table, I get off the bed and walk over to him, wrap my arms around his waist, and rest my head on his chest. "Love you, big guy. I'm sorry."

He wraps his arms around me and squeezes, breathing in deeply before letting it out. "That's all right, babe. I'll think of a way for you to make it up to me." He pulls away and swats me on the ass, and a yelp escapes.

Dudebro and Uptight both grimace and adopt identical disgusted looks.

Snapping my fingers, I conjure a gag onto Dudebro's mouth and turn to Uptight. "Not a word unless Maddock whispers something to you. You can say hello, welcome them to the interview, and then introduce me and announce that I am in charge of person-nel, so I will be leading the meeting. Understand?"

He nods quickly in agreement, and we head out of the room, flicking the do not disturb sign into place as we leave. Hopefully, by the time we are done this afternoon, we will have a few more staff.

CHAPTER
Eleven

Tatiana

"Now, this is more like it," I exclaim as we get out of the hovercar when we arrive at the fae market.

On the edge of the city, the market is a bustling hive of activity. There are many different creatures in several different shapes. Much like a produce market on Earth, the stalls look to be a temporary setup. As we start walking and exploring, Tempest explains that the different vendors come and go depending on season and supply. Earthy animal smells fill the air, and the noise of various creatures creates a cacophony of sounds that resonates through the marketplace.

We walk past one vendor who has hairy creatures in some pens. They are similar in size to sheep, but unlike wool, they have long shaggy fur. The fur comes in a multitude of colors, and some of them even have an ombre variation. They have paws instead of hooves, and they have horns like a goat, but their head is cat-shaped with cat-like eyes. I can see a few fangs when one of them yawns in my direction. I watch as two short, ugly men argue next to them. They are not much higher than the animals themselves, and the conversation looks to be heated.

Tempest notices that I have stopped to watch, and she comes back.

"They are called rainbow lekida. The ones that have the ombre fur are quite rare and prized. The problem with breeding them is they aren't guaranteed to throw ombre color. They may just be plain. There is no rhyme or reason to the coloring, it's just magic."

It looks like the two men come to an agreement, and both spit in their hands and shake on it.

"They are dwarfs. They are the only ones who the lekida will thrive for. Every other species that has tried to breed them has failed. It's almost like they have a symbiotic relationship, who knows, but the lekida fur produces the most marvelous fabric. It's spun and then woven, and it is so soft, like a cloud. It's like you're not wearing anything, but it's tough and won't rip, and it regulates your body temperature. You can wear the skimpiest dress in the snow, and you will never feel it, which is very handy for the noble fae who try to wear as little as possible, as often as possible." She rolls her eyes, and we keep walking.

We make it a little bit farther, and I stop dead, my mouth dropping open. The inner little girl inside me starts screaming and jumping up and down in delight.

"What? What's wrong?" Tempest comes back and throws herself in front of me, looking for danger, a sword manifesting in her hand out of nowhere. Hmm, maybe it wasn't just my inner little girl screaming.

"Unicorns!" I scream and point at the horses in a nearby arena.

She stops and looks at me. "Really?" She lifts an eyebrow and drops her hand, the sword disappearing.

"Yes, really! You have no idea. That, there, is my dream animal." I'm so excited, I'm almost hyperventilating.

She grabs me by the hand and tows me over to the pen. Standing next to it is a female fae with long blue hair in a single braid down her back. She's dressed in leather riding pants and a corset top. She turns and greets us with a huge smile on her face.

"Tempest!" she exclaims. "I wasn't expecting to see you today." They hug each other, lingering a little longer than what's considered friendly. Hmm.

"This is Tatiana from the Arbor Vitae Coven," Tempest says, giving introductions. "This is my friend Elliot Stormrider. Ellie is the alicorn herd master."

I look over their shoulders, and sure enough, they are not just unicorns, but they have wings as well.

"Be still, my beating heart." I clasp a hand to my

chest in excitement. "May I please pet one?" I beg Elliot.

She smiles indulgently at me. "Of course you can, just come up to the fence and wait. The alicorn picks the person. They are very particular." I walk up to the fence and pray to my goddess that one comes over. It would suck to be rejected.

"So I heard rumors about a joint venture between the fae and the Arbor Vitae Coven. Does this mean they are true?" Elliot leans against the fence next to me, and Tempest joins her.

"Yes. Tatiana is here with Regan Miller. He's up at the palace having a meeting with the king and council."

I turn to them in shock. "That tower is the palace?"

They both laugh, and Elliot scrunches up her nose. "Is Aven in the meeting too?"

Tempest rolls her eyes. "Yes, unfortunately."

"Well, I'm sure that's going to go well," Elliot says sarcastically. I make a note to remember to ask Regan about these comments, not wanting to interrupt.

I watch the alicorns while Tempest and Elliot whisper between themselves, but I don't feel like I'm left out, just that they have their own private stuff to talk about.

The alicorns are similar in color to horses back on Earth, but it's like the color is permanently in high definition. It's somehow brighter and more vibrant than earth tones. As I watch them graze, the herd parts, and from the middle, a gangly golden alicorn with a black mane and tail prances in my direction, snorting and throwing his head in the air. The girls stop talking, and we watch as the regal creature comes toward us. Mesmerized by the sight, we watch in shock as he gets his hooves tangled and stumbles over them, ending up on his knees in front of us. Elliot snorts and bursts into laughter.

"Is it okay?" I ask in concern.

"Yep, that's Sunstorm. He thinks a lot of himself. Usually, his father puts him back into place." She nods at the big black stallion that is watching the proceedings. He looks like he's rolling his eyes at his colt.

I watch as Sunstorm gets back to his feet, and at a more sedate pace, steps in front of me and shoves his nose under my armpit, almost taking my eye out with his horn. Dodging it quickly, I notice that it has a rubber ball on the tip, stopping it from causing any damage. I slowly raise my hand and rub him between the ears around the base of his horn, and he starts to purr like a kitten.

"Why is that on there?" I ask, gesturing to the ball, noticing that none of the others have it.

She snorts. "Because he's not the smartest alicorn. He's like a teenage boy with too much testosterone. He does stupid things and gets stuck places. This morning, I found him with his horn stuck in a tree trunk, unable to move. It was the last straw. Now he must suffer the indignity of having that on."

"Oh, poor baby," I coo to him, and he pulls his

head back and nickers into my chest before lipping at my shirt.

"Well, that's that then. Thank the goddess! I thought I'd be stuck with him forever. He's such a disaster waiting to happen. Where shall I have him delivered?"

I turn to her in shock. "What... What do you mean?"

"He's yours now. That's how it works." Tempest sighs. "Shit, the head groomsman is going to kill me. Have him delivered to the royal stables. You can keep him there until he's been trained. You'll have to make frequent trips to work with him, and Ellie will help you." She turns to the fae. "Won't you?" Elliot nods her head and smiles.

"I'll have the money transferred to your account," the princess tells her. "We'll call it a gift toward realm relations."

"But... But..." I stammer as Sunstorm steps back from our cuddle and decides to prance up and down the fence line. He spreads his wings out and waves them. His wings are black, just like his mane and tail, and the span is enormous.

"As you can see by his wingspan, he's still got a bit to go before he is fully grown. You can't ride him until he is, but you can train him to take the saddle and bridle and work with voice commands."

"What am I going to do with an alicorn?" I sputter.

"Visit the fae realm regularly." Tempest grabs me by the arm and starts to drag me away. "Come on, we need to get going, otherwise, you won't find what you need. I'll see you later, Ellie." We wave goodbye to the herd master and keep walking.

Tempest hangs onto me because she knows I'm in shock. We hurry past more weird and wonderful creatures, but I'm too dazed to pay attention.

Finally, I snap out of it as she brings me to a halt in front of the fruit and vegetable section filled with shouting fae and strange and delightful smells.

"So what are you looking for? Do you want something sweet, tart, or sour? And do you want it to have an effect or be benign?"

"An effect or benign?" I question, not understanding what she means.

She drags me over to a stall with a small pixie woman sitting in front of it. "This is joy fruit." She picks up the little magenta-colored fruit. It's similar in size to a kiwi, but instead of being furry, this has scales like an artichoke. "It gives you a feeling of pure joy when you eat it."

"Is it addictive?" I ask her, taking it from her hand and bringing it to my nose to smell it. It has a smell that is a cross between a strawberry and a mango.

She shakes her head. "No, not addictive at all, just fun." She hands a coin to the pixie lady. "Here, you peel back the scales." She takes another one and shows me.

Once peeled, the flesh is the same color as the scales. I take a bite, and a burst of flavor coats my tongue. It tastes exactly as it smells, but it has a bite of sourness when it first crosses your taste buds before fading to sweetness.

"This is perfect," I tell her, wiping a drop of juice from my chin. A huge grin crosses my face. I have a new fruit, an alicorn, and a new friend. Could anything make this day better?

The pixie lady hands us both a little tablet, and copying Tempest, I slip it into my mouth. The feeling of joy fades away.

"Oh, wow, that's amazing."

"I'll give you the recipe for the antidote," Tempest says, pointing to her mouth. "You can give them away with the ice cream. Sometimes it's needed quickly, and it's a requirement to sell them with the fruit."

Thanking the lady, we move on. The next stall she brings me to has a long fruit shaped like a cucumber, but it is orange in color with sienna spots. Again, she hands over a couple of coins to the creature operating the stall. This one is wearing a little red hat and has ruddy cheeks. I think he's a gnome.

Handing me one of the fruits, she shows me how to peel back the leather-like exterior. The fruit inside is shockingly blue, and it looks like pomegranate seeds.

"Try it." She shows me how to scoop the seeds out. "This one is benign, it's just a fruit," she assures me.

Shaking off my concerns, I scoop out some of the seeds. I place them in my mouth and roll them around on my tongue before crunching down on them. They taste like a cross between a coffee bean and chocolate. There's a bitter bite and then a mellow sweet flavor. "What's this called?" I ask, scooping more into my mouth.

She laughs, and a slight blush stains her cheeks. "They have a fae name that translates into moon rods."

I look at the phallic-like fruits and join in her laughter. "These are great, Tempest. Thank you. I already have some ideas about what to do with both fruits."

"Actually, there is one more stall I want to take you to. Galan was telling me all about your difficulties on Earth and how you think there is a spell on you and your friends to keep you away from the island."

I nod my head and follow her toward a little permanent building with a sign above it reading, "Potions." A bell tinkles above the door as we walk in.

"He told me about the spell your mothers did to break it, but it wasn't as effective as you hoped it would be."

When we walk up to the counter, we are greeted by a gorgeous man with spiky purple hair, sharp cheekbones, a welcoming smile, and silver eyes as ancient as the mountains. "Princess Tempest, what a delight to see you today." He leans over and places a lingering kiss on each of her cheeks, causing another bout of pink to bloom. "And who might this be?"

"This is Tatiana, the witch I was telling you about.

This is Master Alsorin, the best potion maker in the fae realm." His silver eyes look me up and down, seeing far more than I am comfortable with.

"Ah, yes. The one from the coven that seems to have a hidden enemy." He turns and heads into a back room before returning with two flasks. The first one is a little gold, conical-shaped bottle.

"This is a spell breaking potion. There is enough for the ten of you who need to have the geas broken. It's rare, which is why I can't give you enough for all the townspeople, but with the ten of you returning, nothing will get in your way. Take your dose now," he insists, pulling a thimble-sized glass out of thin air, placing it on the counter, and pouring the potion in. It glimmers gold as it trickles into the glass.

I pick it up and down it in one go. It almost makes a reappearance at the taste, but I grit my teeth and get it down.

My surprise at his knowledge must show, because Tempest chimes in. "Master Alsorin is a seer as well. It's what makes him such a great potion brewer. He can see exactly what he needs for the right outcome."

He hands me the second flask, which is purple, tall, and cylindrical. "This one is for your magic depletion."

"Huh?" I ask in confusion, looking to Tempest for an explanation.

"Galan said the spell has stopped you from using

your magic, and your magic muscles have wasted away."

"Oh yes, that's right," I reply. "It causes us to forget we have magic, and we don't use it."

Master Alsorin nods. "Yes, all magic must be used, or it wastes away. It is the same realm wide. Shifters must shift both ways. Vampires must use their heightened senses, strength, and speed, and fae species must use their magic. Anyway, this will give you a boost, and your magic will return instantly. In fact, it may be stronger than normal to start with before it eases. But from what I understand, the ten of you are the most powerful witches the coven has seen since the originals."

My mouth drops open in shock. This is not common knowledge.

"This is why you ten were targeted," he continues. "Someone discovered this. I can't see specifics regarding who, but I can tell you that's why you were singled out and why it makes you forget about your magic. This doesn't happen with the blanket spell affecting the rest of the island's younger generations. Be careful with this. It will be dangerous in the wrong hands." He hands both bottles to Tempest.

"Shall I send these back to the palace?" she asks, and I nod. With a little spark of light, the bottles disappear. "They are in my personal safe at the palace. I'll retrieve them for you when we get back."

"Thank you so very much, Master Alsorin." I hold out my hand to thank him. He clasps it, and his eyes go cloudy and roll back in his head, and his fingers clench down on mine. I freeze and look to Tempest in panic, trying to pull free. "What's going on?"

"Just wait," she commands, and I stop struggling. "He's having a vision."

We wait for what seems like hours, but is really only a few seconds, before his eyes clear and focus.

"Be wary. Whoever is behind the spell is not the only one you have to worry about."

"Can you tell me anything else?" I demand, but he shakes his head.

"No, sometimes the visions are specific and sometimes they are vague. I just got a feeling this time."

My heart drops with disappointment. "I understand. Thank you for the warning and the potions."

He turns to Tempest and grabs her hand again, placing another kiss on it. "I'll be seeing you soon, Tempest Silvershadow. Say hello to Elliot Stormrider for me." He winks and disappears into thin air.

"Damn show-off," she grumbles. "Come on, let's get some lunch. I need a drink."

CHAPTER
Twelve

Tatiana

Tempest takes me to a fae tavern for lunch. While we are walking, we're stopped regularly with people greeting the princess, waving, and saying hello. She's gracious and patient, even though I know she really wants a drink after our encounter with Alsorin.

When we finally make it to the tavern, it looks like something out of medieval England with large, stone building blocks and a thatched roof. It has a sign on the side that says "The Flaccid Slug," with what looks like an inebriated caterpillar drawn next to the name.

Huh, that's an um… interesting name.

We walk in, and the roar from the patrons when they see the princess is loud and jovial. Mugs of beer are raised in a toast and shouts of "Cheers!" ring through the building. She smiles and waves in return, and they all turn back to what they were doing. A gap in the crowd is made as we make our way to the front. When we get to the bar, a short man with pointy ears, a large bulbous nose, and a pointy chin smiles and shouts in greeting. "Princess Tempest. What brings you to our humble abode this fine day?"

"Corym Meadowmead, it is a two-pint day," she declares as she drops onto a vacant stool.

"Oh dear, let me get right to it." He hustles toward a beer tap at the other end of the bar.

"Get one for my friend too," she shouts to him, and he nods, grabbing another tankard. "Corym is a clurichaun—a type of leprechaun who specializes in alcohol and brews the best fae cider throughout the whole realm. It's made from the joy fruit and has a two-pint limit, but I think we deserve the treat after our busy morning and Alsorin's dire warnings."

"Hmm, yes, his warning must be the reason for the pints. Not the sexual frustration that's dripping off you." I take advantage of the opening to quiz her. "I noticed that both Elliot and Alsorin were very excited to see you."

Corym comes back and puts the tankards in front of us. "Oh ho, both Elliot and Alsorin in one day? No wonder you are in need of two." He turns to me. "And let me guess, this is one of the witches from the earth realm here to organize your realm tours."

I hold out my hand. "Hi, I'm Tatiana, and yes, my friend is up at the palace doing that now."

He shakes my hand. "Ah, yes, Regan Miller is a

good man. I've had the pleasure of his company in the past. And I think possibly your brother Maddock, yes?" He raises an eyebrow in question. My surprise must show on my face. "The coven boys used to sneak into the fae realm occasionally and come here and join in the revelry. They were eventually caught by your parents, and a stop was put to it, but hopefully, with this new accord, I will see them again. They were very popular with the fae ladies."

Hmm, interesting. Maddock has some explaining to do. I wonder why we never heard of this and why the hell we weren't invited too?

I take a sip of the cider and swallow before coughing at the potency. A slight buzz hits me instantly, but it's not as extreme as when I bit into the pure fruit.

He gestures to a jar of the antidote pills sitting a little farther down the counter. "Grab a couple for later."

I stick a few in my pocket.

Feeling good, I start to grill Tempest regarding her friends. "So, tell me all about Elliot and Alsorin."

She's already downed half her drink, and she wipes her mouth on the back of her sleeve before she answers. Wow, Tempest is not the dainty fairy princess I thought she was. "There is nothing to tell. As a princess of the realm, my destiny is set, even if I have found my mates. I will marry to further our political alliances, or that's what my brother will have me do."

"I thought he was still the crown prince, so why can't your dad overrule him?"

"It's a transition period. That's the deal Father struck with Aven. Unfortunately, Aven… How do I put this diplomatically?" She stops and looks around, but no one is really paying attention. "Screw diplomacy. He's a dick, and what's worse, he is a dick with substance abuse problems. Dad really doesn't want to hand over the reins, but it is a diplomatic minefield that he is treading very carefully, so he allows Aven to make these decisions for now." She gulps down the rest of the pint before slamming it on the bar. "Hit me again, Corym."

"So are you saying that Elliot and Alsorin are your mates?"

Before she can answer, a shout and a flash of magic draws our attention to the other side of the tavern. The crowd surges toward the commotion, and Tempest and I join them when Corym bolts over the bar and pushes his way through. When we get to the front of the crowd, a fight has broken out, and it's like it's contagious—every new person who stops and looks gets drawn into the fray. Fists are flying, tankards are smashed over heads, and bodies are thrown onto furniture. Whatever is affecting the patrons grabs hold of Tempest too, and with a battle cry, her sword appears in her hand and she jumps into the skirmish.

It seems like Corym and I are the only two not affected. I shoot him a questioning look, and he holds up a charm around his neck. "I need it to keep my business safe."

Nodding, I turn back to watch the brawl. I guess Alsorin's potion must be protecting me.

Finally, it seems to run its course. There are bodies strewn all over the floor of the tavern, and in the epicenter of the fight is a small circle of charred floor, littered with little shards of purple glass.

Corym grunts in disgust. "Looks like someone dropped a spell. This will take all day to clean up. Alright, everyone out," he shouts to the still conscious patrons. "Make sure you drag an unconscious body with you. Drop them at a medical center if you are not willing to take responsibility. And if I ever find out who was so careless as to drop that spell, it will be a lifetime ban."

The crowd disperses, picking up unconscious bodies and hauling them over shoulders or supporting dazed companions. They trickle out until it is only Tempest, Corym, and me left. The princess's lovely silver dress is missing a sleeve, and she has blood splattered across the front. Her sword has gone back into the ether, but there are no dead bodies left behind, so thankfully she didn't kill anyone.

I try to snort back a laugh, but I can't stop it, and it explodes from my lungs. Bending in half, I hold my stomach. "I thought you were a dainty fae princess. Boy, was I wrong."

She flips me a finger and climbs back onto a stool next to the bar. "I didn't get my other pint, Corym."

"Be off with you," he demands. "You made a lot

of this mess too. Princess or not, unless you're going to stay and clean, get."

Grumbling, she gets up and stomps out. Thanking Corym and waving goodbye, I hurry after her. She is in the process of waving down what looks like a hover taxi. One stops in front of her, and a high-pitched buzzing noise can be heard emanating from the pink glow. We climb in, and it takes off.

"What's that noise?" I ask, the pitch grating against my nerves.

"The damn noise-canceling tech must be broken," she complains.

I laugh at the grumpy princess. "So I guess something like that cancels out the joy properties of the cider?" I ask.

"Yes, damn fool carrying a spell like that in a crowded area."

My buzz continues as we head back to the castle, and the thought of seeing Regan makes everything awesome.

Once we return, I am shown to a room to rest and freshen up before dinner with the royal family. Regan is still in meetings with the prime minister, so I won't see him before dinner. After having a little nap, I use the fantastic facilities I have been given. The shower is like standing under a natural waterfall. Although the buildings are very modern and luxurious, they seem to have found a happy medium with lots of foliage and natural fittings inside.

Drying off, I walk into the wardrobe to find something suitable to wear. As I examine the rack of dresses, I hear a knock on my door and shout, "Come in," before continuing my perusal.

"I brought your potions over for you." Tempest stands in the doorway of the closet. She's wearing another long, silver, corseted dress with strategically placed pieces of fabric. The rest of it is gauzy and flowing.

"Seriously? What's with all these dresses?" I gesture to the pieces of fabric hanging on the rack. "We have strippers on Earth who wear more fabric."

She moves to the rack and pulls out a scrap of emerald and tosses it at me. "Suck it up, buttercup. Isn't there an Earth saying? When in Rome? Put that one on and come out, and I'll do your hair."

"A princess doing my hair? Isn't there a maid for that?"

"There is, but it relaxes me, and since I was cheated out of my joy-joy cider, this is the next best thing, especially since Aven will be at dinner too." She leaves the closet, and I put the dress on.

It actually isn't as bad as I thought. It's not see-through like hers, though the neckline plunges to my navel and has a front split that sits just under my crotch. I'll need to make small, ladylike movements so I won't flash anyone my goodies this evening, but I don't feel overexposed.

Walking into the bedroom, I sit down in front of a mirrored cabinet, and she starts brushing my hair.

"We're friends now, right, Tatiana?" Tempest asks me quietly. Her eyes have a slightly haunted look when I catch her gaze in the mirror.

"Of course we are. You bought me an alicorn. We're BFFs as far as I'm concerned." I shoot her a wink in the mirror in the hope of easing her worries.

"Well, in honor of our friendship, I will ask you to please not let yourself be alone with my brother tonight." She turns me around and grabs me by the arms. "Promise me."

I'm pretty sure she's going to leave fingerprint bruises on me, so I quickly nod my head without asking any questions, and she lets out a relieved breath before turning me back toward the mirror.

"Okay then." With quick and practiced move-ments, she has my hair twisted and pinned before I can blink. She then moves to the other flask of potion I haven't taken yet and pours a shot into a glass. "Take this too," she demands, handing it to me.

Remembering the taste of the last one, I screw up my nose but do as she bids. This one bubbles across my taste buds, light and fruity, and a wave of magic courses through my body. I feel invincible. 'Whoa!"

Her body relaxes even more. "Good, I won't worry so much now. A magicless witch in the fae court is not safe, especially a beautiful one."

I put on the pair of heels I selected and give myself a once over in the mirror.

"You look hot. Regan won't be able to take his eyes off you."

"Oh, it's not like that," I sputter, not sure who I'm trying to convince.

She rolls her eyes and ignores me. "Sure, sure," she says as she throws open the door to the suite.

Dinner is an intimate affair. Tempest introduces me to her mother and father. Regan and Aven are already seated, and Tempest steers me to the spare seat next to Regan. On my other side is her uncle Helio, the prime minister that has been in meetings all day with Regan. I am introduced to the few other people at the table. On Regan's other side is the prime minister's daughter and Tempest's cousin, Bumble, whose large breasts are pressed up into a shelf under her chin, and her long eyelashes keep fluttering in Regan's direction.

There is also a thin, pale-looking lady sitting next to Aven, who is introduced to me as Antoinette. Aven tells me she is the vampire ambassador to the fae realm. She whispers, "Hello," but keeps her gaze down, then she jumps as a plate of food is put in front of her.

Tempest takes the seat on the other side of Aven and flags down the waiter who placed the plate of fruit in front of Antoinette. "Could you grab the ambassador a glass of blood too, please? She is looking a little pale this evening."

The vampire's head comes up, and her mouth drops open in shock. A grateful look briefly crosses her face before she carefully blanks it and nods her head toward Tempest in thanks. Aven's hand tightens on the goblet he's holding, his knuckles turning white, the only outward sign that he is not happy.

I feel a hand on mine under the table. Looking down, I see Regan giving it a warning squeeze. Hmm, all is not right in the realm of the fae. I wonder if Galan is aware. When I look up at Regan, he briefly shakes his head, and I pick up my knife and fork and start my dinner.

Conversation quietly flows as dinner is consumed. It's all benign and harmless little bits of palace gossip, or questions aimed at Regan and me regarding our realm.

Just as we finish dinner, a mischievous expression crosses Tempest's face. "Regan, wasn't there somewhere you wanted to take Tatiana this evening?"

His face lights up, and he wipes his mouth with his napkin. "Yes, there is, thank you for reminding me, Princess." He turns to the king and queen. "Thank you for the meal. Would you mind excusing us?"

King Florian smiles. "No, not at all, and you are very welcome. We will say goodbye now as I know you have to return early tomorrow morning. We look forward to continued and improved relations with Arbor Vitae Coven."

Queen Selene also wishes us luck.

Regan takes my hand, and we leave the dining room. Tempest waves in my direction and throws me a wink. "Have fun."

Aven has a scowl on his face and stays silent on his side of the table.

As we enter the elevator and head down, I finally get a chance to take a breath. "Where are we going?" I ask him, but he smiles secretively and shakes his head.

"It's a surprise."

Downstairs, the same limo we used this morning is waiting for us, and we climb in. It pulls silently away from the curb, taking us to the mystery location.

"Have you had a good time?" Regan asks as we get comfortable. "I haven't had a chance to ask you yet. Was your trip to the market successful?"

I bounce up and down on the seat in excitement. "Oh my goddess, yes! Tempest bought me an alicorn."

Regan does a double take, looking shocked. "What?"

"I was looking at the alicorns while Tempest talked to her friend Elliot, and one walked right up and chose me. She's going to keep it at the royal stables for me, and I'm going to travel back and forth to care for it."

"Wow," he says in amazement. "Not many non-fae can claim to own an alicorn. Please don't tell the children, or they will want one too."

"Why not? There is room at the manor for one," I ask, laughing.

He shudders. "Yes, there is, but I'm not sure airplanes would cope very well with an alicorn's flight pattern. We would have to make the island a no-fly zone." We both laugh at that, and I tell him about the two fruits I have decided to use in my recipes.

"I'll let Helio know that you're going to place regular orders that will need to be delivered to the portal," he tells me as the limo glides to a stop.

CHAPTER
Thirteen

Regan

It took all my self-control to hold myself in check during the drive. Tatiana looks ravishing in her fae dress. The swollen tops of her breasts are accentuated by the long V-neckline, and every time she moves her legs, I get a tantalizing glimpse of her underwear through that slit. I just about swallowed my tongue when she first arrived at dinner, and I thank the goddess that Tempest directed her to sit next to me instead of that evil fucker Aven.

Helio told me some hair-raising stories during our time together, and I couldn't believe the audacity he had to bring the vampire ambassador to dinner. Ambassador my ass, more like a concubine. I can't believe the king allows that behavior. Thank goodness steps are being taken to change the line of succession, although anything less than a sword through the heart is too good for that asshole.

Stepping out of the limo, I hold my hand out to help Tatiana. Another flash of her underwear teases my senses before she straightens herself out.

"Where are we, Regan?" Curiosity fills her voice.

Shaking my head to clear my thoughts, I hold out my arm. She takes it, and we start to walk forward.

"This is a fae botanical garden. It is right in the center of the city. It's similar to Central Park in New York, but this one has a special function."

The warm air is perfumed with intoxicating scents, and the evening is balmy and tropical as we walk past weird and wonderful foliage and flowers. Her exclamations of joy and amazement ring through the canopy as we explore this fascinating place.

I wanted to do something special for Tatiana, so I organized to have it closed off to the public this evening so that we may enjoy it privately. We stroll the meandering pathways for quite some distance before we get to the main attraction.

In this part of the garden, the lighting is minimal, and there is a viewing platform. I stop her on the platform and turn her to look over the little glade it towers over. Stretched out as far as the eye can see are thousands of bright little lights in a rainbow of colors flittering to-and-fro amongst the foliage. It's a tiny wonderland of a village to invoke the inner child in everyone.

"Wow, Regan." Tatiana sighs. "It's beautiful. They look like fireflies. What are they?"

A few start to fly a little closer when they hear her voice.

"They are fairies," I tell her, watching as the hand she was starting to hold up comes to a dead stop.

"What did you say?" she asks, panic entering her voice.

"Fairies. Like Tinker Bell," I reply. This time I do not imagine the panic that crosses her face.

She pulls away from me, and in shock, I watch as she starts to wave her arms at them like she's a ninja on the attack. "Shoo, shoo," she shouts. "I can't believe you brought me here," she screeches.

My heart drops, and I try to stop her from touching the fairies. "Don't touch them, Tatiana. They are harmless, they won't hurt you, but you shouldn't touch them."

I grab her around the waist and pull her body into mine, whispering in her ear. "Don't move a muscle," I warn her.

She stops instantly when I command it, and the caveman in me roars at her compliance. Shit, that didn't help with my dick problem.

Too late. The irate fairies start to buzz like a swarm of angry wasps, and I watch as we are covered in fairy dust, the angry chattering piercing our ears.

"I'm sorry," I call to them. "You frightened her. She didn't mean it." The chattering eases, and the group flies away from us, but it's too late. I can feel the dust start to take effect.

"Not flesh-eating bacteria?" she asks quietly.

"No," I answer in surprise. "Who told you that?"

"That bitch," she mutters under her breath.

"No. Fairies are harmless unless their dust touches you."

She starts to squirm in my arms. "What does the dust do?" she asks, looking up at me, her eyes big and round, the pretty brown pupils blown out.

"It's like ecstasy. This park has orgy festivals during certain times of the year. It's a fae fertility thing. I brought you here because I thought you would get a kick out of the fairies. How was I to know Tempest had set you up?"

She rubs her chest against mine and grinds against my thigh. A moan escapes her lips. "Help me, Regan," she begs.

My cock is as hard as steel, and my hands have a mind of their own as they roam over her body. "Shit, Tatiana. I don't want you to hate me for taking advantage of you," I tell her quietly, trying to stop, but I just want to ravish her.

"I won't," she pleads. "I wanted you before the dust."

That's enough for me, and I take her by the hand and drag her a little farther on to one of the cushioned, secluded nooks set aside for precisely this reason. Pushing her down onto the mossy ground, I seal my mouth over hers in a kiss that far exceeds anything I've had before. Our panting breaths mingle as lips and tongues explore each other. Pushing her dress aside, I pinch one dusky pink nipple and roll it between my thumb and finger.

A groan escapes her mouth, and she pants, "More."

Her hand fumbles for my zipper, but I won't let her take control. Using my magic, I summon a nearby vine and have it wrap her hands together before pulling them up over her head. Sitting back on my heels, I run my gaze over her writhing body. Her thighs rub together as her big doe eyes look up at me, pleading for me to ease her ache.

I snap my fingers, and she's instantly naked. My dick throbs at the sight. Tatiana has long, elegant limbs with shapely breasts and hips. A neat strip of curls at the junction of her thighs draws my gaze. I summon two more vines, and they slither out and wrap around each ankle, drawing her legs apart and exposing her glistening pink pussy to my eyes.

"Is your pretty pussy wet for me?" I growl, and she whimpers in response. My mouth waters, and I lean down and run my tongue from her dripping entrance to her clit. The musky taste of her explodes across my tongue, and we groan in unison, her gasping, "More."

Settling between her legs, I feast on her, drawing deep moans from her mouth, her pleas causing my cock to weep. Thrusting my tongue in and out, I mimic what my cock will be doing to her very shortly. I move up to her clit and replace my tongue with two fingers, thrusting them in hard and fast, not giving her any chance to adjust as I lap at her clit like a cat with cream.

The groans that come from her mouth are music to my ears. Her pussy starts to tighten around my fingers as her moans increase in volume, and I know she's close. With one last thrust, I suck hard on her clit, and she detonates like a rocket, screaming her pleasure to the world. Her juices soak my hand, and I continue to thrust slowly as she rides out her orgasm.

Not giving her much time to recover, I slide up her body, her skin smooth and soft against mine. Taking one nipple into my mouth, I swirl my tongue around the bud before giving it a gentle bite. I give the other nipple the same attention before moving up to her mouth and kissing her, letting her taste herself.

Without pulling away, I line myself up and thrust hard into her hot, wet, spongy heat, and a long, loud groan escapes my mouth. Her pussy is still pulsing and has a vise-like grip on my cock. Holding still for a moment, I take a deep breath to center myself, then I start to thrust, flexing my hips as I pound into her body.

I snap my fingers to release the vines around her ankles then reach down, grab her thigh, and hike her leg up over my hip to give me a deeper angle. Our gasps, grunts, and groans fill the evening air, and the smell of sex surrounds us. I can feel her body building to another climax, so I speed up, using long, deep strokes to hit the spot inside her that brings such delicious sounds from her mouth. Her gasping increases, as does my speed. My name falls from her lips as she pleads for more.

The tingle at the base of my spine threatens to erupt, but I hold it back, gritting my teeth until I feel her explode around my cock. Struggling, I thrust through her orgasm, and finally, with one last plunge,

I moan her name as my cum fills her tight wet channel.

I wait until our bodies finish shuddering before I roll to the side, sinking down in the mossy ground. Releasing the vines around her arms, I drag her against my body. Both of us are covered in a sheen of sweat, and our breathing is still uneven as I massage her arms to help with the blood flow. Pushing her damp hair back off her forehead, I place soft kisses all over her face. Her eyes drift closed, and a gentle smile curves her lips.

"Wow!" she breathes. "I've never… That was…" Her husky, addled words cause my cock to harden against her thigh as she snuggles into me. Her eyes pop open. "Again?" She sounds a little incredulous, and I laugh as I drift my kisses lower toward her beautiful full breasts.

"It's the dust," I mumble as she starts to pant again and grabs my head, holding it in place as I suck on one and then the other nipple.

She grinds her mound against my thigh, and a breathy, "Oh," escapes her mouth as I flip her over onto all fours.

"I hope you don't want any sleep," I warn as I watch my cum drip out of her pussy and onto the ground below. I run my hands over the round globes of her ass before I swat one of the peachy mounds. A yelp escapes her mouth as I watch a pretty red hand-print bloom on her delicate skin.

After pausing for a second to rub away the sting, I swap to the other side and repeat the movement. The rush of seeing my mark on her makes my dick throb with impatience. Grabbing hold of her hips, I thrust deep without any warning.

A loud moan escapes her mouth, and she demands, "More." She's a wanton goddess at my command.

CHAPTER
Fourteen

Tatiana

anging on the door wakes me. I open my eyes to find the morning light creeping through a gap in the curtains. Groaning, I try to roll over, but a hand has me pinned firmly to the bed, and that's when I remember. I turn my head. Regan looks peaceful in sleep, his disheveled hair sticking out at all angles.

When we got back to the palace, we showered together to wash off the remaining fairy dust, which led to more fantastic sex that carried on throughout the night. Although the side effects of the dust eventually eased, the ache between my legs is set to remind me for days to come. I have never seen such stamina.

Another knock on the door draws my attention, and Tempest's voice rings out. "I just wanted to remind you that your jump is in an hour. Better get a move on. I'll be waiting by the elevator at ten minutes to ten. Don't be late."

I try to escape Regan's clutches, but he tightens his grip and pulls me closer. When I roll back to look at him, his green eyes sparkle, but a frown creases his brow.

"No regrets?" he asks, sounding a little unsure.

Shaking my head, I place a soft kiss on his lips. "Absolutely not," I assure him. "In fact, let's see if we can smuggle some of that home." I wink at him, and he covers my mouth in a long, lazy kiss, bringing goosebumps to my arms and legs and causing my nipples to pucker in excitement.

"We don't need to smuggle it," he murmurs when he pulls away. "You can buy it in potion stores and at the market. Tempest probably didn't show you because she told you that they had flesh-eating venom." Between the rounds of sex last night, I told him how she had convinced me fairies were bad, and he had a good laugh.

An idea hits me. "I might make it an adults-only ice cream for Valentine's Day. I will layer a spell on it, so it will only work on people who are attracted to each other and would normally consent. That way, we don't have any cases of date rape."

His hands start to creep lower, and his hips thrust, rubbing his cock against my leg.

"Hang on, Romeo, I don't think I can take anymore today. How about we grab a quick shower before the jump?"

He places another quick kiss on my lips and

jumps out of bed, walking naked toward the bath-room. His ass is tight enough to bounce a quarter off of. Who knew he had such a ripped body? He's long and lean like a swimmer with bulges in all the right places. Thinking about his Adonis belt makes my mouth water, and I hurry after him.

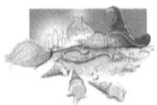

After a not so quick shower, where he proved I could take more, Regan and I both hurry to gather our things to make the jump through the portal. We are both out of breath by the time we get to the elevator.

Tempest arches a brow at me. "Late night?" she questions, tongue in cheek.

"Listen here, bitch." I take a step forward, but Regan puts a hand on me, and she dissolves into peals of laughter. "You'll keep," I tell her. "Karma is a witch who has been wronged."

"But were you really?" she asks. "Didn't Regan warn you of mischievous fae?"

I look at him, and a guilty look crosses his face, then he pulls me into a hug. "I'm sorry, baby," he apologizes. "I've been so damn tired it slipped my mind."

My anger dissolves at the warm words and endearment. "It's okay, no harm was done."

"No, from the looks of it, only good things

happened," Tempest chimes in as the elevator comes to a stop.

We all step out just as the portal bursts to life. Not wanting to waste time, we hurry toward it. I promise Tempest to return soon to look after Sunstorm.

"You better," she tells me, "or I will be the one coming to get you."

Waving goodbye, we step through the portal holding hands, the cool, damp mist surrounding us for the few steps it takes before we walk out into the coven waiting room—where we find one of Regan's replicas and Julie wrapped in a passionate embrace. Again! Julie's leg is wrapped around his waist, and his hand is creeping its way up her skirt.

"What the holy hell is going on here?" Regan bellows, dropping my hand and pulling the two apart. I wince. Shit, they got away from Ruby again. This one is wearing a suit, but the minute he opens his mouth, I realize it's Dudebro Regan.

"Chill, man, way to cockblock a friend."

If the situation wasn't so serious, I would have grinned at the incredulous look on Regan's face. Who am I kidding? I totally smile, and a snort may escape too. Regan sends me a dirty look, while Julie has a look of stunned surprise as she glances between the two. "But, but, but…"

"I think you guys have broken her," I remark, grabbing her by the arm and propelling her toward the elevator. "Bring him with you, and I'll explain on the way."

Regan yells into the control booth where William

is watching, his mouth open in surprise. "Cancel the vampire jump and inform them we have been delayed. We will make the next jump for twelve."

William shuts his mouth and nods before pushing buttons on his computer in front of him.

Grabbing Dudebro by the arm, he joins us in the elevator, and I press the button for the correct floor. "You know about this?" he growls at me, and I hold my hands up in defense.

"This is all Ruby!" I tell him. "I had nothing to do with it. She was trying to help you, but she made a mess of it. Her intentions were good, so think about that before you get too mad."

He stews as the elevator rises to the right floor. I drag Julie with me, and Regan and Dudebro follow until we get to Room 119. The door is wide open when we arrive, and Ruby and Maddock are standing over a naked, semi-conscious replica. He sits up, looking around in a daze.

Her head shoots up as we pile into the room, and I pull the door closed behind us. "Why you little…" She lunges at Dudebro and wraps her hands around his throat.

He struggles to free her as I watch on in amusement. Regan jumps in and pulls them apart before shoving Dudebro away.

"Ruby, what the fuck is going on?" he shouts at her.

"Fuck." She drops into a chair, looking exhausted. She runs a hand through her pink locks. "I am so tired," she complains before taking a deep breath. "So the interviews went well. Uptight Regan sat quietly and did as he was told. Today's round was a success. But when I sent him back to the room in the evening, he fell for dickhead's sob story and untied him. Dudebro proceeded to knock him unconscious and steal his clothes. He said he's been gone all night."

We all turn to Dudebro and Julie, and a sick feeling fills my stomach. He has a smug look on his face, and she has stubble burn on her neck and cheek.

Does that count as cheating? I think to myself then shake my head at the ridiculous thought when I remember how my night had gone. I smirk at the justice of her getting the watered-down version of Regan. Feeling quite smug, I cross my arms and continue to observe.

"Ruby, where did they come from?" Regan waves his hands at his two replicas.

"A spell," she mumbles, "and the blood from the napkin at dinner the other night."

Regan looks dumbstruck. "Ruby, you have done some stupid things, but I think you just outdid yourself."

Her whole body slumps. "I know." They both stand there looking exhausted, and I decide it's my turn to step in. Taking Regan's arm, I push him into a chair next to Ruby, then I put my hands on his shoulders and rub.

"Okay, we all agree that what she did was stupid, but like I said, she did have good intentions." I watch Regan's eyes drift to my cleavage, which is now near his face, and I smirk. There's his man-whore side. He sees my smirk and grins at me. Placing a quick kiss on his lips, I turn back to face the room.

Ruby's and Maddock's mouths have dropped open, and they are looking between the two of us in surprise.

"When did this happen?" my brother asks, gesturing between the two of us, but I wave him off.

"We'll tell you about it later. What are we going to do with these two? There really is no need for them to be here for the interviews since Regan is still going to have to meet the new employees anyway. Are you sure there wasn't anything in that spell book for getting rid of replicas? I'm sure we can't be the only ones to have problems with them."

Ruby holds out her hands, and a large spell book appears in it. She flicks through the pages, and I go over and stand behind her. She stops at a page and points. "This is the spell I used."

Leaning over, I read the page. When I pass the section about a time frame, I spot a tiny segment at the bottom. "There." I point to it.

A sheepish look crosses Ruby's face. "I was so excited about the spell I guess I didn't read any further." Her head smacks down onto the tome. "Christ, I could have saved all my troubles."

Turning to the two replicas, I lift my hand and wave it at them. "Retexo!" Dudebro leaps at me, but it's too late, and they both slowly dissolve sort of like all those superheroes at the end of that movie.

Ruby stands up and sends the book back to where it came from. Dusting her hands off, she declares,

"Well, that's that. No harm, no foul." The three of us look at her incredulously.

Shaking my head, I gesture to Julie. "What are we going to do about her?" She's been watching with fascinated curiosity. I had seen her eyeing the spell book like it was the Hope Diamond.

"Nothing," Regan replies, and he stands up. "I'm sorry for what occurred, Julie. Please return to work." She looks between the four of us.

Nodding, she turns to leave the room. "Of course."

"Oh, and Julie," Regan calls, and she stops dead. "You were in a restricted area of the manor without permission. It's a fireable offense. I'll overlook it, but in return, I'm going to ask you not to mention anything that happened here."

She nods her head slowly and continues on her way.

I can't believe he is being so trusting, so I whisper a little spell and send it toward her. A small wave of light covers her briefly before sinking into her skin. Regan looks at me with a raised brow. "You're too trusting. Remember, we still aren't sure of her origins yet, though with her interest in the portal, I'm going to say they are suspicious. Now she definitely won't say anything."

"Okay, we need to get back down to the portal room and make our way to the vampire realm." Regan retakes charge.

"Just let me run upstairs and grab something," I

tell him. I can see Ruby's brain whirling, so I decide to get out before she asks any questions.

A gleam enters Regan's eye, and he says, "I'll come with you." I do a double take. I saw that same gleam in Dudebro's eye. Oh yeah, I know why he wants to come with me. Waving goodbye to the other two, we walk out hand in hand to the sound of Ruby's splutters and Maddock telling her to leave us be. I love my big brother. I owe him one now.

When we arrive at my room and push the door open, I'm giggling with anticipation. Regan didn't exactly keep his hands to himself in the elevator, but the sight that greets us stops that instantly.

My room is trashed. Clothing is strewn from one end of the room to the other, and it looks like it didn't survive destruction either. The mattress, pillows, and cushions are all shredded with feathers and stuffing all over the room. The petals from the rose I received the first night are ground into the carpet, and the TV screen has been smashed—the chair sitting underneath possibly the reason.

I gasp, and Regan pulls me close while grabbing his cell and quickly typing a message. Not long after he returns it to his jeans, Ruby and Maddock rush in.

"Whoa," Ruby exclaims. "Who did you piss off?" Maddock shoots her a dirty look, but she just shrugs.

A laugh escapes as I pull myself together and out of Regan's arms. "Who knows?" I reply. "Maybe Julie, but apparently she was busy all night." We all look at Regan, and he blushes. "It wasn't me." He holds his hands up in defense.

I search through the scattered clothes, looking for a fresh pair of undies. Regan ripped a pair last night, and I have on the only other pair I took with me. Obviously, I wasn't thinking clearly when I packed. Finding one that seems to have escaped destruction, I shove them into the pocket of my jeans and turn around.

"What are we going to do?" I ask, feeling helpless.

Ruby comes over and gives me a hug. "I saw that," she whispers in my ear. "I want to hear all about it when you come back." She frowns slightly, then shakes her head. "Well, most of it anyway." Pulling back, she says louder, "Go, we've got this."

Pulling the potions out of my backpack, I hand them to Ruby. "These are important. Can you put them somewhere safe, and I'll tell you about them when we get back?"

She takes them, promising to put them in the coven vault.

Regan doesn't even argue, just grabs my hand and drags me out. Before I know it, we are back in the portal room with the vampire realm coordinates loaded into the computer.

CHAPTER
Fifteen

Tatiana

Regan's friend Cole meets us on the vampire side of the portal. "It's a pleasure to finally meet you, Tatiana. I've heard many stories regarding the Tempting Ten."

Rolling my eyes at that ridiculous name, I return his greeting. He leads us from the cold, damp portal room and into what looks like an honest to God castle. Looking around in amazement, I interrupt whatever Cole is saying to Regan.

"Now this is what I was expecting the fae realm to look like." Looking around a large common room, I see elaborate tapestries on the wall covering the stone building blocks. The furnishing is very medieval England style with lots of carved wood. Rugs are spread across the floor, and a fire blazes in the fireplace on one wall, but it's not putting out enough heat to warm the vast room. A shiver runs down my back, and a cold chill permeates my bones as I shuffle closer to Regan, crowding him for his body heat.

Cole frowns as my teeth start to chatter. "Sorry about the cold. Vampires don't feel temperature, so we forget until we receive visitors." He snaps his fingers, and a fur coat is wrapped around my shoulders. Turning, I thank the pretty girl who is now handing one to Regan.

"Come, my cousins are waiting," he tells us as he leads us through the vast room.

Following him down a couple of corridors, we are stopped by a set of guards in front of massive wooden double doors. Cole gives them a nod and pushes the doors open to a large throne room. The smell of fire and smoke fills the air from the many fireplaces dotted along the walls. They must be for ambiance, or maybe they lit them for us. This room is much warmer than the first one we were in.

As we walk the immense distance between the doors and the dais at the front, I allow my eyes to wander. We are surrounded by many vampires, all beautiful, elegant, and deadly. Lounging on strategically placed couches, they project a casual air of relaxation, but I can see by the tension in their muscles and the calculating looks in their eyes that they are ready for anything. They silently follow our movement across the room.

As we approach, my eyes return to the raised dais. Sitting on it are three thrones filled with three very similar-looking men. The men must be related, and when I look from them to Cole, I can see a familial resemblance. These must be his cousins. Regan never mentioned how well connected he was. All three of them have dark hair of various lengths and matching, eerie bright blue eyes. Blank faces greet our arrival.

We stop directly in front of the group of men. "Cousins, Regan has brought a friend with him. May I introduce you to Tatiana Crane. Tatiana, may I introduce Kings Jacob, Jett, and Jeremiah." He gestures from left to right.

Regan nods, and I attempt a little curtsy, not knowing the correct protocol. I'm going to kick his ass for not warning me that Cole's cousins were the kings.

Their blank expressions turn into bright grins as all three get to their feet and move down the stairs to shake hands with me. They are welcoming, warm, and inviting. As they do a bro-style back slap thing with Regan, I turn and observe the observing vampires. They have now all relaxed, and the noise of their conversations reaches my ears as they proceed to ignore us now that their kings have welcomed us so warmly.

"Come," Jett says, tucking my hand under his arm and escorting me up the stairs. "Let us move to a more comfortable and quiet area for our conversation."

We follow the three men up and over the dais to a door, manned by a guard, behind the platform. We follow him through to a more intimate meeting room with a bar on one side and a small, comfortable seating area. Jett guides me to a sofa and releases my arm, bowing slightly to me.

"Tatiana, it's a pleasure to meet you. We have heard much about you from Maddock over the years." Hmm, another thing Maddock and Regan need to explain. I had no idea they were all so familiar with the other realms.

"Thank you for having us," I reply politely. Drinks are handed around, and we all take a seat. I listen intently to the plans for the tours to the vampire realm.

The tours will include the option to be bitten if the tourist is so inclined, as well as a visit to the Enarac Grove.

"What is the Enarac Grove?" My curiosity gets the better of me.

"What do you know about vampires?" Jeremiah asks me.

Blushing slightly, I admit, "I know you need blood to survive, have enhanced strength, speed, and senses, and that the sunlight thing is a myth, as is the stake in the heart."

The vampires all nod their heads encouragingly.

"You have instant healing, and drinking blood has a regenerating effect on your blood cells. Oh, and you are born, not turned, though you have the ability to turn a mate if they desire. If the mate is a supe, they will retain their birth nature but also take on vampire characteristics. You develop normally until your twenty-fifth year when you go through your vampire awakening. All children born with at least one vampire parent will go through an awakening and will need to drink blood to satisfy that need, though they will also retain the characteristics of their other parent." Hmm, I actually knew more than I thought.

He smiles, pleased at what I have said. "Don't be ashamed, you know most of it," he reassures me. "We eat food, but you're right, vampires need blood to survive. However, unlike Earth legends, it doesn't need to be human. Don't get me wrong, human blood is a delicacy, as we don't have our own human population, but we can drink from other vampires and supernaturals. When we find our mates, we are then restricted to just drinking from them. Vampires are fine once we mate, since we overproduce blood to provide for our mate, but if our mate is a different species, they won't produce enough. This is where the enarac fruit comes in. It is an enchanted fruit that they need to eat every day to increase their blood production."

"Oh, wow, that is very cool," I tell them.

"It is. It was gifted to us from our goddess when interspecies mating started occurring after we had some near tragedies. Although most mates choose to transform, for some reason, the blood production still isn't enough," Jacob expounds. "But apparently it's not very nice tasting."

"How does a vampire know when they have met their mate?" Regan asks curiously.

"Usually through intimate contact. It's why vampires are such a promiscuous lot," Jacob answers, laughing. "Except for Cole here. He's a little more discreet than most."

"That's because I'm too busy chasing off your rejects after you hit it and quit it because they are not your mates," he grumbles. "A lot of female vampires don't care and would settle to be one of the kings' playthings." His cousins look a little embarrassed by this comment, but then a sly look crosses Cole's face. "But what all these females don't realize is that these three are closet romantics and are desperately searching for their *one*."

The three kings grumble at his words, but none of them deny it.

"You know, I can probably work out a way to turn the fruit into ice cream and maybe make it more palatable," I suggest, changing the subject.

Jett's eyes light up before dimming again. "No, we've tried mixing it with things, but it doesn't seem to work."

"Yes, but you don't have magic." I wiggle my fingers at them. "I'm sure someone in the coven has the knowledge we need to help you out."

"Tatiana, if you could do that, there are many vampire mates who will worship the ground you walk on, and we would immediately place orders with you. In fact, if it works, how about we negotiate for you to set up a factory here in the vampire realm? It will make you a wealthy woman," Jacob says, throwing out a tempting offer.

"I don't need to be a rich woman, but I am sure we can come to some type of agreement."

Another vampire comes into the room from a side door. "Please have some enarac fruit delivered so that Ms. Crane can take it back to Earth with her."

"How are you going to create the recipe without tasting it?" Regan looks at me with concern.

"Well, I planned on tasting it," I tell him, confused by his worry.

"But what about the extra blood you will produce? That can't be good for you," he argues.

"Oh, I hadn't thought about that." I look at the kings. "Will it hurt me?"

"Probably not, but you can taste it here, and Cole or one of us can bite you if you want," Jett offers with a twinkle in his eye.

"Over my dead fucking body!" Regan roars, leaping to his feet. The four vampires look at Regan in surprise.

"Man, it's okay. Calm down," Cole cajoles. "We didn't know that you were together, sorry."

Regan backs down slightly.

"What's the big deal?" I ask, surprised at his violent reaction.

"Biting leads to orgasms," Jeremiah tells me, grinning at Regan.

"Oh. I guess that's one of the things I didn't know." I laugh softly and reach up, putting my hand reassuringly on Regan. He takes a deep breath and sits down next to me, grabbing my hand and not letting go.

A gleam enters Jacob's eye. "We could let him take the potion," he suggests to his brothers. Grins cover the mouths of Cole and the two other brothers.

"What potion?" Regan and I ask together.

"We have a potion, again gifted by our goddess. Deciding to transition to a vampire is a big decision for a mate to make and irreversible once done. She didn't want any mate to regret their choice and created a solution. The potion changes the person into a vampire temporarily for a couple of hours, allowing them to experience all the changes to their body as well as giving them fangs and the ability to digest blood. It's a try before you buy option. We could give Regan the potion, which would allow him to drink the excess blood from you."

"Whoa, now that I definitely didn't know," I say, looking at Regan who shakes his head. He didn't know either. My body is suddenly racked with desire.

"It is a closely guarded vampire secret, and one we trust you will keep to yourselves," Coles tells us with a serious look on his face.

We both nod in agreement.

"Can we both eat the fruit and both take the potion?" I ask in the hope that it's possible. I would love to know what being a vampire is like.

They all look at each other like they are having a private conversation before Jett nods his head. "I don't see that being a problem. You're going to be doing us a huge favor. Cole, can you show them to a private room?" We stand up to follow him.

"Before you go..." Jeremiah stops us. "Did you

happen to see Antoinette, our ambassador, when you were in the fae realm?"

Fuck! My heart speeds up, and I hope they think it's because I'm excited to try this potion, and not because of their question. Regan and I look at each other before he answers.

"Yes. She had dinner with us last night, in fact," he replies.

"Her reports have been very brief recently. Did she look okay to you?" Jacob asks, the concern in his voice evident.

"She was very quiet," I tell them, and the three kings look at each other in surprise. "Really?" Jett asks. "That's not like Nettie at all."

Crap, a nickname. They must know her well.

"Maybe once the portal is operational again and realm access a little more flexible, we will pay a visit to the fae realm ourselves," Jacob declares. "We can check on our people there."

With nothing more to say, we follow Cole to our designated room.

"Do they know the ambassador well?" I ask him on our way.

"Yes, we all grew up together, but the three of them were always very protective of her for some reason."

"Oh, romantically?" I inquire, digging for details.

"No, much to her disgust." He laughs. "But they were always very respectful. It hurt her to see their man-whore ways, so that's why she asked for the ambassador position."

"Shit!" Regan stops him with a hand on his arm. "You need to have her recalled. Things are going on in the fae realm at the moment, and it would be better if she returned home until they have been sorted." It seems like Regan has heard more than the vague warnings Tempest gave me.

Cole looks between the two of us and nods his head before continuing on to our room.

CHAPTER
Sixteen

Regan

Our room looks like it's set up for an orgy, but I guess it could be knowing what I now know about vampires. The bed is large enough for five full-size people to spread out on, and it's covered in dark satin sheets. Large pillows are scattered around the room with other unusual surfaces with chains and rings and ribbons attached to some of them. Gauzy drapes hang strategically around the room, and it looks like they can be used to divide it into sections, and one portion is surrounding the bed. Cole told us to make ourselves at home while we wait for the potion and the fruit to be delivered.

Tatiana drapes herself across a chaise that I suspect is used for ménages because it has her at the right height to suck my cock—which is trying to force its way through my zipper at the thought.

Not wanting to get interrupted once we start, I keep my hands to myself and pace the room, waiting for our delivery. She has an amused look on her face and starts to strip her clothes off while I watch.

"Are you a bit worked up, Regan?" she asks as she pulls her shirt over her head, leaving her sitting there in a sexy red lacy bra and black jeans. She pulls the ponytail holder out of her hair, and it tumbles down her back in a waterfall of lush, chocolate locks.

Impatience and need get the better of me, and I start to pull my own shirt over my head without unbuttoning it when a knock at the door has me stopping. I open it to find Cole standing there with the vampire from before. He has two weird-looking pieces of fruit in his hand. The size and shape of a plum, they have a smooth surface like an egg, but ironically enough, they are blood-red. Cole has a flask in his hand.

The servant hands them to me and walks away.

"Crack them in half and eat the fruit inside," Cole tells me. He walks to the bar in the room. Glancing toward Tatiana, I can see she has pulled her shirt up in front of herself, covering her breasts. I breathe out a sigh of relief, not having to worry about my jealousy getting the better of me. He pours a shot of the potion into two small glasses and pops the stopper back on.

"Now you can't drain each other dry due to the fruit, but I don't recommend biting each other more than once or twice just to be on the safe side. Give it half an hour for the fruit to work before you take the potion," he warns us as he heads for the door. "Have fun." He winks and pulls the door closed behind him.

Leaving the potion where it is, I head over to the chaise and offer her a little round egg. Cracking it on the coffee table close by, I pull the hard casing apart. Inside are two slimy globs of fruit that look a little like blood-red balls of snot.

Tatiana wrinkles her nose then leans down and takes a sniff, pulling away with her eyes watering. "Oh God. No wonder the mates don't like taking it. It smells like dirty socks and looks disgusting." She cracks hers open too.

"Okay, on three," I tell her. "One, two, three."

We both slide first one and then the other into our mouths like oysters and quickly swallow them down.

Tatiana's gag reflex kicks in, and she slaps a hand over her mouth as a green tinge settles on her cheeks. "That was disgusting," she complains when she finally gets control of herself. "It tasted like moldy cheese and sweaty gyms socks fucked, and that was their baby," she grumbles, throwing herself back on the chaise.

Laughing, I pick her up in my arms and carry her over to the orgy bed. I lie down and wrap my arms around her, placing her head against my chest. We lie there quietly for a minute. Having her in my arms feels amazing.

"What are we, Regan?" she asks, and my heart speeds up. Okay, we're going there. "Not that I'm trying to put a label on it or anything, but are we going to continue this back home? Are we telling people or hiding it? Mostly I want to know if we are going to tell your children." The words leave her mouth in a nervous rush.

I take a deep breath and let it out. She starts to pull away, but I hold on tight. "I would like to continue this. I have no intention of hiding it from anyone, my children included, as long as you are comfortable with that," I tell her, and this time I do let her pull away. I want to see her face when she responds.

"Really?" she asks, sounding unsure.

"Absolutely! As long as you're aware, and I know I don't have to say this to you, but my children come first every time. They have been let down by one parent, and I refuse to put them in that situation again."

She smiles and places a gentle kiss on my lips. "Oh, Regan, that goes without saying. I'm looking forward to getting to know them better though." Her smile turns into a frown, and she brings up the subject I've been dreading. "What are we going to say if they ask us about the ambassador again? I don't know the full story, but something fishy was going on, wasn't it?"

I pull her close again, needing to feel her warmth. "Yeah." I blow out a big breath, and it ruffles her hair, so I run my hand over it, smoothing it down. "The fae are working on it. We have to trust that they will find a solution. Helio assured me a plan was in place. Look, I don't want to talk about it too much because I don't know how much privacy we actually have, but the fae will do everything they can to avoid war."

I decide to change the subject.

"Come on." I pull her to her feet. "Let's have a bath together." I drag her up and into the sumptuous bathroom that I know is attached to this room.

All marble and gold fittings, the bath is sunken down into the floor in a small pool. Sandalwood scented steam fills the room, and jets bubble low in the water, sending ripples across the surface of the pool. Tatiana gasps at the sight as I start to slip her out of the rest of her clothes. Unzipping her jeans, I crouch down to draw them down her legs. As she steps out of them, I place a kiss at the junction of her thighs over her panties, inhaling the heady aroma that is her.

My cock roars back to life, and we both hurry to remove our clothes. I lunge at her and throw her over my shoulder, smacking her on the ass before stepping down into the pool. Her giggles echo through the room until I get to the middle and slowly slide her body down mine until she is face-to-face with me. Our lips collide in a slow and sensual kiss, our tongues tasting and teeth nipping before we pull apart and find a seat together around the edge.

Tatiana groans as she sits down. "Oh my god, this feels so good. My body has been aching all day. You really worked it over last night."

I can feel a smug smirk cross my mouth. "You're damn right I did." She laughs at the pride in my voice and snuggles in close. I wrap an arm around her shoulders and hold her tight. "This was a great idea."

"I don't think I will come with you to the shifter realm," she says after we sit here in contemplation for a few minutes. "I have a couple of new fruits from the fae realm and the fairy dust to create with. I'm also doing this one for the vampires, plus I'm going to give the marijuana ice cream a go as well as a few of the alcoholic cocktail ones I want to create."

"They do have some interesting native fruits," I comment. "I bet the merpeople would have something remarkable, but their realm is the one that is most similar to ours. Did you know they actually have a fruit that allows you to switch what animal you can change into? It's temporary and restricted to shifters who have control of their shift, but maybe when you get a chance, you could do something fun with that." I kiss her temple.

"Merpeople?" She groans. "Damn it, I really want to go now, but I need to get started, plus I have to finish the haunted house plans. Tell me more about shifters. I don't think I know as much about them as I do vampires."

"Shifters recognize their mates by scent, which triggers their mating mark. They are also governed by a supreme alpha. Did you know there are mythical creature shifters too?"

She shakes her head, her eyes wide in amazement. "Tell me all about them," she demands, and we spend the next twenty or so minutes talking about the shifter realm.

I stop when I realize Tatiana is squirming, and it doesn't have anything to do with me. "Are you okay?" I ask her worriedly.

"I feel like my skin is too small for my body. There is this feeling of pins and needles all over me."

Standing up, I reach for her and carry her out of the pool. Using one of the towels, I dry us both and then take her to the bed, placing her down gently.

"I only feel a slight buzz," I tell her, going over to the potion. "Maybe it's because I'm bigger than you." I hand her one of the glasses, and we clink them together and down it quickly. A shudder spreads through my body as the coppery taste explodes across my taste buds.

Tatiana groans. "That one doesn't taste any better," she complains as I walk across the room to put the glasses back.

Suddenly, she becomes completely still. A wave of magic flows over her body, and her pupils shrink until they are only a pinprick before they dilate completely, smothering the beautiful blue in her eyes. She shudders and doubles over groaning before she bolts upright with fangs now in her mouth, her nostrils flaring as she eyes me like I am the next thing on her plate.

Before I can say anything, I feel the wave flow over me. Grunting with the pain, I manage to stay upright as it feels like my entire body cramps. My eyesight disappears before returning with amazing accuracy. The sound of her heartbeat thunders in my ears, and the smell of her desire just about knocks me off my feet. The throbbing in my gums is the only warning I get before my fangs punch through, drawing a groan from my mouth.

I take a step toward her and instantly move from where I am to on the bed in front of her. Her shocked face must mirror mine.

I look to where I just was. "Huh. Wasn't ethpecting that," I lisp around my fangs. Tatiana's shocked expression turns to one of pure mirth. I can see her struggling, but the laugh escapes.

"Oh my god, that wasth stho funny." She claps a hand over her mouth, and her eyes widen.

"Mm-hmm, not so easy, is it?" I say slowly, avoiding the fangs in my mouth. I breathe in, and again her scent is potent in my nostrils. I groan, pulling her toward me.

The feeling of our naked bodies sliding against each other is sweet torture as all our senses are in overdrive. Our mouths come together in gentle exploration, not wanting to cut each other with our fangs, but they seem to have receded back into our gums, so our kisses turn more urgent.

I lay her back on the bed and trail kisses down to her breasts. I circle first one nipple, then the other with my tongue, and my fangs snap back into place. I graze her nipples with them, and she squeals in surprise then shudders in delight.

"More," she moans.

With her hands in my hair, I trail down her body, but she suddenly stops me. Quick as a flash, I find myself on my back with her hovering over me, her knees on either side of my body.

"Wow!" The look of shock on her face is funny. "Vampire strength rocks."

Before I can say anything, she slides down my body, and her tongue glides over one of my nipples. The wet heat and suction goes straight to my cock, causing it to jump. She moves farther down, trailing open-mouthed kisses down my body. I hold still, my hands wrapped in the sheets as anticipation keeps me on a knife's edge.

Finally, she gets to my cock and runs her tongue from base to tip, dipping into my slit and scooping up the trail of precum. A hum of enjoyment escapes her mouth as she closes it around my tip. The feeling sends a pulse through my body.

The scrape of her fangs on my cock has me grunting in both want and worry. I allow her to lick and suck momentarily, the overabundance of senses a riot in my mind. Stopping her before it can go further, I pull her up my body.

"I'm not so sure we should get too carried away with these fangs in sensitive spots," I mumble into her ear as I roll her over onto her back.

Lining up at her entrance, I thrust hard, sliding into her wet heat and seating myself balls deep. We both groan in unison. Not waiting for her to adjust, I set a steady pace. Our collective moans of pleasure are a symphony in the air. For what seems like hours, we draw the pleasure out of each other's bodies. Staring into her eyes, I see my reflection in the dark pupils, the look of pure passion growing with each pounding thrust. Her mouth is open, her pants are music to my ears, and her fangs are down and ready to strike.

The tingle at the base of my spine signals my impending release, and when the fluttering of her pussy gets too intense, I strike. I instinctively know exactly where to bite, as does she as I feel her fangs pierce my shoulder. The release is beyond anything I have ever felt. My body is moving faster than it ever has, but she screams, demanding more, before she latches back onto my neck. The sucking sensation of her mouth feels like it has a direct connection to my cock, and with every pull, I pulse another stream of cum into her. Her blood is like liquid fire flowing through my system, like a fine whisky, warming and potent, and it fills my soul.

Her feelings echo through my body. Her pleasure is mine and mine hers in a never-ending reciprocal cycle. The orgasm slowly fades, as does the urge to drink, so after licking the wound, I let go. Her tongue swiping against my neck tells me she is doing the same thing before we pull apart and collapse next to each other.

"Wow," she whispers, her breathing slowly getting back to normal. "Thank goodness for coven birth control. Otherwise, the magic from the last two days would have really screwed us over." She laughs, and a slight hitch in my heart tells me that even if the birth control didn't work, I wouldn't be too worried. Pulling her close, I run my hand up and down one of her arms, drawing goosebumps to the surface, and she giggles.

"That was amazing. I wonder if many mates reject the change? I wouldn't." My hand goes down and smacks her ass, and she yelps before quickly saying, "Not that I'm not completely happy, but do you think we can convince the kings to let us occasionally vacation here without the children?"

I laugh at both what she is saying and at the wonderful fact that she is already including my children in her life. She rolls over, and I cuddle into her from behind, the big spoon to her little spoon. "Baby, I think if you can provide them with ice cream from the fruit that makes it taste good, you can be a part-time vampire whenever you want."

Her sleepy response brings a sense of warmth and contentment to me. "Only if it's with you, Regan."

CHAPTER
Seventeen

Tatiana

T he next morning, we are up early to have breakfast with the kings and Cole since we missed dinner with them last night.

The vampires are full of suggestions and innuendos. It's amusing watching them rib Regan. It's like seeing a group of frat boys talk about who got lucky last night. Both Regan and I have a well-fucked look about us. The fangs were gone, but we made the most of that big bed this morning. I'm not ashamed at all, and I have already negotiated regular vacations that include fruit and potions with Jett.

"Tatiana, do you think you could create blood ice cream as a treat for us as well?" Jacob asks me. "While you are experimenting with the fruit, could you experiment with that?"

I think about it. "I can give it a try, but to do that, I would need a constant supply of blood, and I am not sure that is practical. And to be honest, blood is warm, and ice cream is the exact opposite." His hopeful look drops, and I feel a little guilty. "Leave it with me, and I'll see what I can do. I may be able to find a spell to help."

He seems satisfied with that.

"Regan, when can we expect the portal up and running again?" Jeremiah inquiries. "We have some vampires in the human realm who need to return, and Cole has something to check on Earth."

"Within the week, I would expect," he tells them. "The power fluctuations seemed to have stopped, so all travel can resume as normal."

I'm about to mention the power I felt the other night while growing the corn that seemed similar to the portal, but we are interrupted as a vampire guard enters the room. "The portal is activated and waiting for them, sir," he reports to Cole.

Standing up, we thank the kings for their hospitality and follow Cole to the portal room.

"Tatiana," Jett calls, and I turn to face him. "I know your coven are honorable people, so if you would like to tell your friends about the potion, we won't be upset. Oh, and please inform your brother there will be a room waiting for him and Regan's sister when they are ready." He winks, and within a blink of an eye, the three of them disappear.

That's a relief. I was wondering how I was going to avoid Ruby's third degree, but now I can tell her everything.

We wave goodbye to Cole, with him telling us

he'll see us soon, and then we step through the portal again. I instinctively brace myself for what we will find on the other side, but the waiting room is empty, and we can only see Mac in the control room. A big sigh escapes both of our mouths, and we look at each other in relief.

"Thank goodness, I'm too tired to cope with any Ruby drama today," Regan mumbles as he pushes his hands back through his hair. "One more to go. I'm going to get this wrapped up as soon as possible so I can come home to see you and the twins. Don't make any plans tonight. We will tell them about us."

A flash of nerves buzzes to life in my stomach, but I shake them off and give him a kiss goodbye. "Be careful. I'll miss you." I stand and watch as the vampire portal is closed, and the shifter one flares to life.

I wave as he steps through before heading toward the elevator. Thankfully the biometric scanner is only for people coming down from the top, and I'm able to make my way back up into the hotel.

Hitting my floor, I stroll out, looking forward to getting a shower in my room when I pass the closet I was dragged into by Dudebro Regan and I hear another noise coming from it. Suspicious, I peer around it when an arm snaps out and grabs hold of me, dragging me into the dark depths. Fuck, not again. I thought we had vanquished them. Getting ready to turn around and knee him in the balls, I feel my heart rate skip a beat as a hand clamps over my mouth and a familiar voice whispers in my ear.

"What have you done to me, bitch? You lying little whore. Have you put a curse on me, witch? I can't get you out of my head." Marco's accented voice is harsh in the enclosed space and spittle flies across my face with each whispered word. The light switches on, and my heart just about stops at the sight of a sharp pair of scissors in his hand.

"Marco, what are you doing? I haven't done anything to you," I plead with him.

"Lies," he spits, shaking me hard. "All fucking lies. She told me what to do with you. She told me that a lock of hair was all she needed to remove the curse. Imagine what she could do with all of it." With that, he hacks away at my hair. As the first chunk hits the floor, I remember my returned magic and blast him away from me with a wave of my hands just as the closet door flies open and Regan bursts in.

"Praestringo!" he shouts, and the cord from the vacuum cleaner in the closet slithers out and wraps itself around Marco. Regan pulls me into his arms where I burst into tears, relieved at seeing him.

"I don't know what's gotten into him. He was never like this before." I sob, my tears wetting his shirt as he holds me tight. A noise behind us draws our attention, and we turn to find Ruby and Maddock staring at us.

"What's going on?" she asks, stepping out of the way so we can get out of the cramped closet. Regan leads me out and then goes back in to help Maddock bring out a struggling cursing Marco. The wave of Italian out of his mouth is not pleasant, and I cringe.

"Marco has gotten it into his brain that I have cursed him or something and had been informed by someone that they needed a lock of my hair to break it." My hands go up to feel the damage, and I discover a section sitting above my shoulders. My heart drops.

Regan sees my reaction. "Baby, long or short hair, you are still beautiful to me."

A grin crosses Maddock's face at Regan's words before he turns hard eyes on Marco.

"I thought you had gone through the portal," I say to Regan. "How did you get here so quickly?"

"I had, but the potion must still be affecting us slightly, because I felt your heart skip a beat and how terrified you were all of a sudden, so I raced back. I'm just sorry I wasn't quick enough."

Ruby has her phone out and is telling the sheriff what has happened and to expect Marco shortly. She hangs up and turns to us. "If this is not like him, maybe this is the fallout from the spell," she suggests.

We all watch as his ranting starts to turn to gibberish and foam begins to froth from his mouth. Ruby waves a hand, and a gag silences him, putting an end to his tirade. "Anyway, the sheriff is expecting him."

I watch as she waves her hand, and he disappears. Knowing that Taylor is going to deal with him is a huge relief.

Regan grabs my hand and pulls me close again. "I don't want to, but I really have to get this shifter visit finalized. Are you going to be okay?"

"Of course she is," Ruby assures him. "We will sort out the mess he made of her hair, and she will be right as rain again."

So again, we part ways. Ruby walks with me to my room, and Maddock goes with Regan.

"Do you think it was Marco who trashed my room?" I ask her quietly.

"I have no doubt now," she replies. "Oh, and the rat. I didn't think Sugar would slit its neck and leave it for you. Was there anything else strange?"

"There was the rose on my pillow when I first arrived, but I assumed it was the turndown service, and my notebook with my recipes was not where I left it."

She laughs. "Ah, yeah, we don't have a turndown service at the moment."

"Well, I guess that was him too," I tell her. "Speaking of that, how did yesterday's interviews go?"

"Great, we filled a few more positions, and the last ones are today. We can then have a meet and greet for Regan to approve them all, and then we should be back in tip-top shape," she says as we get to my room and open it up.

Looking around, I can see it is back to the way it was, and with the blessing that is magic, all of my clothes have been repaired and are stacked on my bed.

Ruby throws her ass down on it and looks at me. "Start talking," she demands, and a small smile crosses my face.

"Just let me get a shower, and then I'll tell you everything," I promise her.

So that's what we do. I spend the next couple of hours telling Ruby about my and Regan's adventures in realm travel and romance.

That afternoon, while Ruby conducts the rest of the interviews, I teleport into town and have my hair fixed at the local beauty salon. I cry while the hairdresser cuts off the rest of my hair, but she does a really great job at styling it, and I'm happy with the flippy, flirty look. When I walk out, my hair feels so light, I feel like a shampoo ad, tossing my hair back and forth. I've had long hair for as long as I can remember, but it's going to be so easy now that it's shorter.

After popping into Dreamy Delights to check on the renovations, I head back to the manor to sit down and work out my recipes. A note slipped under my door has me worried for a moment, but it's just a note from reception telling me that a couple of boxes of fruit have been delivered from the fae and vampire realms, and that they are in the manor walk-in fridge when I am ready for them.

I have decided not to do anything fancy with the fae fruit and let their own flavors speak for themselves, but the vampire blood snot—as it shall be known from here on forward—is problematic. I have to think about intense flavors to cover that taste. It will require some experimentation. Thinking about using a masking spell, I conjure up one of my parents' grimoires to have a look through.

Flipping through it quickly, I find the one I want. There is one spell that is designed to hide the taste and smell of poisons in food and drink, but I think it may be suitable for this application too. I write it down in my notebook, and with a flick of my hand, I send the grimoire back to where it came from.

Next, I do some research on marijuana ice cream and find one that seems like it would work and taste pretty damn good.

Moving on to the haunted house, I order some decorations and organize for some actors from the drama department of Queen's University in Kingston to come in and play monsters dotted through the manor and maze to scare the patrons. I speak to Bram and Gerald about making us a hot cider stand and a food stand to sell roasted chestnuts. Lastly, I order a bucket load of candy from Candy Connections to give out to the people who attend.

Adding that last thing to my notes, I look at the time on my phone and realize that Regan should be back soon. Not wanting to miss out on spending time with him and the children, I close my notebook and head downstairs to work on the cornfield.

As I look at my progress, I am pleased with how it is going. Realistically, I could grow the thing in seconds now, but it's not needed for another couple of weeks, so I will continue to do it bit by bit. When I'm happy with today's effort, I decide to head in and wait for Regan where it's warmer, but a pair of hands around my waist stop me before I can. I smile as a pair of lips nibble my ear and whisper sweet words to me.

"Wow, look at my sexy girlfriend and her new haircut."

Turning to face him, I place my hands on his shoulders and lean in for a gentle kiss. "How did it go?" I ask when we pull away.

"All locked in and ready to go. The tours are going to be a blast, and hopefully, I have all the checks on my computer so I can send out the first round of invitations tomorrow. But enough about work. Let's head over to my mom and dad's and pick up the kids and take them out for dinner." Hand in hand, Regan and I walk to his car and head out to pick up the children.

Dinner is a rowdy affair peppered with questions about the realms from the children. Neither of them seem too concerned when Regan tells them about us dating, so we will see what happens. When we take them home and put them to bed, they demand that I stay for the story and give them both a kiss goodnight, so I would say I am quietly hopeful.

Regan invites me to stay, and to say I wasn't tempted would be an understatement, but he looks exhausted, and I know if I remain, sleep will be the last thing on his mind, so after a few lingering kisses, I leave.

CHAPTER
Eighteen

Tatiana

The following weeks fly by, and before I know it, it's the thirty-first of October. Shouts and screams echo throughout the manor and outside in the corn maze as people are teased and spooked by the fabulous haunted house we have designed. Murder rooms, cobwebs, mummies, and monsters are placed strategically throughout the manor to maximize anticipation and create an exhilarating interactive experience. Goody bags are placed in the center of the maze to reward those who make it all the way through.

There are people everywhere, much more than just the population of Morbank Island. The ferry has been going hard all day, bringing people here, and the manor rooms are filled for the night. The lines at the cider and chestnut stands are long, and as they wait, they chat about how wonderful everything has been.

The portal is fully operational again, and there doesn't seem to be any issues with the power fluctuations, but I could swear that while I was out here last night doing my final designs on the maze, I could feel the buzz of it again, except that can't be right.

Ruby told me although it is staffed at night, it very rarely operates after nine in the evenings. It had to have been close to midnight when I felt the residual magic.

All staff positions have been filled except for the stables, but Jandar assured Regan he was still happy to look after our horses for the time being.

Speaking of horses, I've been back to the fae realm to see Sunstorm a few times. That has been fun, and although he is still a show-off, we have bonded nicely, and I can't wait for him to finish growing so we can start flying lessons.

The tour guests are here and ready to start their realm jump in a few days. Regan is escorting the first couple, but after that, he is hoping to hire someone we can trust and rely on to continue to take them.

The kids and I aren't going to see him very much, even though the tours return to the manor each evening. But instead of staying with their grandparents, the kids asked to stay with me. I mean technically Regan will be home every evening, but it won't be until late, so I am moving into his rooms while he's gone, which I am quietly excited about. It's temporary, though I wouldn't be opposed to making it a permanent thing.

Dreamy Delights is renovated and fully functional, with a new range of offerings including the two fae fruit and marijuana ice creams. All of which have been hugely popular. We have been swamped for days leading up to the haunted mansion with all the visitors to the island, and so busy that Mom and Melly have both had to put in extra hours to get everyone served and happy.

The coven meeting is in a couple of days, and plans for the open space will be discussed. I'm really looking forward to getting a start on that. Regan mentioned Lucas is making big plans for Thanksgiving and the possibility of using that space to hold it.

We didn't end up hiring a band for the Halloween event. There's enough entertainment, so Lucas said he would get one for Thanksgiving.

"Come on, come on." Kady grabs me by the hand and drags me toward the hayride. Regan, with a toffee apple smeared Kadir, is following closely behind. "We need to get in line, or we will never get our turn," Kady complains.

We join the line. Maddock and Ruby are getting off the one that has just returned, and they look to be the only ones on there. Ruby is flushed, and they both look a little wrinkled with hay stuck in their hair. She has a little lopsided grin, and they join us holding hands.

"How did you manage that?" I ask, gesturing at the empty wagon.

Maddock grins. "I slipped the driver a fifty. I wanted to make out with my girl like teenagers since we never got to do it when we actually were." We laugh and watch as it fills up again. There are too many people, and we have to wait for the next round, much to the twins' disgust.

As we stand there talking about how successful the Halloween celebrations are and how busy both the candy and ice cream stores have been, we are joined by Josh and Galan. They look to be going toward the haunted house when they stop to say hi.

Regan grabs my hand and squeezes it, reminding me not to bring up the fae realm. We made the decision when we returned not to say anything just yet to Galan regarding his brother and the situation. We figured if Tempest hadn't said anything, then she likely wanted it kept secret. Though I did tell him if it wasn't figured out soon, I would be telling him.

Josh and Galan are being regaled by tales of the maze and the prizes in the middle when Cole joins us. Seeing that the children are distracted, he quietly tells us about the investigation he's been doing since he's been back.

"I've been doing a little digging, and I haven't gotten very far, but I was suspicious when I was at the Hamster and Taylor told me he couldn't tell if Julie, Jenna, and that group were supes. To vampires, witches have a certain smell, and I thought it was the same for shifters, but that doesn't seem to be the case. Anyway, I've discovered that Julie and Jenna are witches and they are from the Wives of the Rowan Tree Coven.

"Isn't that the coven that claimed they were the ones who landed on Morbank Island first, so they should be the rightful caretakers of the portal?" Ruby asks Regan.

"Yes. There was a huge argument regarding that, and the covens were prepared to go to war over it, but the goddess stepped in and named the Arbor Vitae Coven as the true guardians," he tells us, reaching over and picking the hay out of Ruby's hair.

"So why would they be here now if the goddess herself stepped in?" Maddock's question has us looking at Cole, and he laughs, holding his hands up.

"Hey, that's all I've got so far, but I will keep digging," he assures us. "It's easier for me to move around and hear things that others can't. I think Mia and Minnie are also witches, but I'm not so sure about Sheree."

We thank him, and he says goodbye and leaves, as do Josh and Galan, leaving the four of us and the twins.

"Hey, how about you ride in the wagon with us?" Ruby suggests to them. "And let Daddy and Tatiana go on their own?" The kids are thrilled at the idea, and I must say I am as well, so when it comes back around, Regan and I climb in by ourselves and lie down amongst the hay, facing up at the stars.

We are dressed warmly, as the evening is bitterly cold, but his body radiates delicious heat, and I snuggle against him. We spend the ride making out like teenagers, but as we loop back for the return journey, something lands on my nose. I look up, and it's like someone has flipped a switch, and down drift perfectly formed white snowflakes. As the ride comes to a stop, Regan helps me down, and we watch as the twins scream and giggle as they try to catch a snowflake on their tongues, and Maddock and Ruby join in.

Now, this is what life should be about—family, friends, and making memories together.

Epilogue

T he snow outside is really starting to blanket the ground as Tatiana, Regan, Ruby, and Maddock are shown into the mayor's office. They take off their coats, gloves, and scarves and hang them on the provided rack before taking a seat in front of his huge desk.

"Thank you for coming to see me," Lucas says as they make themselves comfortable.

"You sounded upset on the phone," Ruby replies, curiosity filling her voice. "What can we help you with?"

"You guys did such a great job on the haunted house, I would like to request your help with the Thanksgiving feast I intend to throw for the town," he answers. "I've drawn up some ideas and plans, and I would love your input, but the main thing I need from you is an introduction to the Lee family."

Ruby and Tatiana exchange a troubled look as Lucas continues.

"I've been trying to get in contact with them about fireworks for the feast, but no one responds."

"Yeah, there's a reason for that," Regan tells him sarcastically, and Lucas looks confused.

"Mr. Lee is a bigot," Maddock states succinctly. "If you're not a witch, you don't matter. Oh, and being a vampire is a thousand times worse. Remember his tirade when Lucas was elected mayor?" he reminds Regan.

"I thought Mom was going to have a fit." Regan shakes his head. "I had no idea the old man knew that kind of language." They both laugh.

"So he's the one I need to convince?" Lucas asks.

"Well, he is the head of the family. His daughter, Fiona, who is friends with my mom, never married, and she had Tia out of wedlock," Ruby informs him.

"Yes, Mom said it was a bit of a scandal. The coven didn't care, but Mr. Lee almost disowned her. It was only through her mother's pleading that she wasn't kicked out," Tatiana adds. "Poor Tia had a very difficult childhood, and being a girl made it that much worse. She really wanted to learn the family business, but Mr. Lee said a girl had no place learning about chemical processes and experimenting with explosives."

Lucas's face is covered in a frown, and his fangs have dropped in his anger. "Racist assholes annoy me, especially ones who have suffered the same treatment. Lack of enlightenment is no excuse."

"She was in LA last time I checked, working for a fireworks manufacturer, but I do know she spent some time in China learning from someone there. If we can get her to return, then your problem will be solved. She will be more than happy to resolve your fireworks issue, plus sticking it to her grandfather would probably be a bonus, especially because you're a vampire." Tatiana's response turns Lucas's frown into a grin.

"I would be more than happy to employ her if you can get her to return," he tells them, glee filling his voice at the thought of causing trouble.

Regan laughs. "Watch it, Lucas, that's not very mayor-like."

Lucas shrugs his shoulders, not giving a damn.

Ruby stands up. "Well, I guess Tia is next on the list. LA, here we come. Oh, and I think Meadow is in LA too. We can kill two birds with one stone."

Bundling back up, they head out into the snow to settle their respective business before making their way to Los Angeles. The thought of two more friends returning puts a spring in their steps.

Thank you for reading!

I hope you enjoyed this book. It would be super awesome if you could leave a review wherever you bought it, because I'd love to hear what you thought of the story.

Acknowledgments

This process doesn't get any easier every time I attempt it. It's frustrating and scary and has me pulling my hair out at times, but it's also thrilling and exciting and has me giggling to myself like a madwoman. The things I'm learning through my characters and their chosen careers is mind-blowing.

Thank goodness for the World Wide Web. That's the internet for anyone younger than thirty-five. Google is my savior.

Thank you to Madura Tea and Bombay Sapphire Gin. This book would not have happened without you.

To Dazed Designs for the amazing cover

And of course Jess from Elemental Editing who made this a much neater book. You're the best, babe.

Coming Soon

Fangtastic Fireworks
Arbor Vitae Coven 3

Prologue

The weather in LA is a lot warmer than Morbank Island when Tatiana and Ruby's plane touches down, and the smell of airplane exhaust permeates the chilly air.

It's early morning, but the sky is already a clear, bright blue, so it should warm up as the day progresses.

They pick up their rental SUV from the counter at the airport and plug Meadow's last known address into the GPS.

"What did Minerva say when you asked about Meadow's whereabouts?" Tatiana asks Ruby as she steers the SUV into the early morning traffic.

"She said Meadow had been in Amsterdam for

about a year but she's now living in LA. She also said there is a possibility she is up north in Eureka. The company she is working for has a marijuana farm up there, but they have retail stores in LA and San Francisco, so she could be anywhere." Ruby's gaze stays on the busy road, but Tatiana can tell that she's rolling her eyes. Their friend Meadow is a little flaky.

"And what about Tia?"

"Fiona said Tia has been all over the world. She was so hurt and angry when Mr. Lee wouldn't teach her the family business," Ruby replies.

"I remember. She said, 'Screw him, I'll learn from someone else.'" Tatiana thinks for a moment. "That was just after graduation. She and Estella were the first to leave, remember? The rest of us didn't until a couple years later."

"She kept in touch with Fiona at first. It must have been before the spell was cast, and they talked all the time. She spent a long time in Australia, learning from one of the great pyrotechnic dynasties there, but then she said the communication slowly dissipated." Ruby shouts some words of abuse at an LA motorist and flips them the finger before continuing. "The only reason she knows where she's been is because she was able to track her with locator spells. Tia went to anyone who would give her a chance. The Lee name gave her an in, and most of them weren't sexist old coots like her grandpa. The last locator spell showed her here in LA, and all it took to find her was googling a few pyrotechnic companies and asking if she worked there." Ruby sounds smug over her detective skills.

"Thank goodness. I thought she might have been in China." Tatiana replies.

They remain quiet as the busy city of LA passes them on their way to their first stop.

Ruby eventually pulls the SUV into a parking bay not far from the dispensary where Meadow is supposedly working. High Hopes is located in an older area that has recently been revitalized, the aged warehouses turned into funky little boutique-style retail stores and cafes.

The words "High Hopes" are painted in neon green, graffiti-style writing in big, bold letters across the front. Nobody can miss the two-story corner building, and it seems to be popular with locals

Music floats out of cafe doors as Tatiana and Ruby walk toward the dispensary. There are a lot of people around for early morning—the uniqueness of the area a draw for tourists and locals alike.

As they get closer, the skunky, earthy smell of weed drifts to their nostrils, and both breathe it in and turn to each other with smiles. Tatiana shakes her head, and Ruby's lips turn down in a pout. "No, we don't have time. Let's get in and find Meadow and then be on our way to get Tia. The mayor needs us back as soon as possible if we are going to organize the Feast and Fireworks for Thanksgiving."

They enter the store, which has classic Bob Marley playing over the speakers. The large, open windows allow plenty of light and fresh air to stream into the store, and the eye-catching displays of various cannabis options draw the eye and tempt the patron. A man who looks to be in his mid-twenties greets the girls as they approach the counter. His faux-hawk is gelled to within an inch of its life and colored a bright neon blue. His eyebrow has a bar through it, drawing attention to his warm chocolate eyes that seem quite clear for someone who works in this kind of business. Maybe it's still too early for him.

"Good morning, ladies. What can I tempt you with today?" His tone is mellow and smooth and could probably tempt you to buy almost anything.

"Hi, we're looking for Meadow." Ruby's voice is bright and friendly, and so is her smile. "Is she here?"

His eyes dim slightly, and he shakes his head. "No, sorry, lovely, but Meadow is up north at the farm at the moment. They had a crisis with a new strain she helped develop, so she flew up there to help out. She won't be back for a week or so."

The girls look at each other in disappointment, thank the guy, then leave.

"Well, crap," Tatiana grumbles as she exits the store. "What now?"

"Don't stress. We're zero for one, but we still have Tia. Let's go get her and then we can shoot up north and get Meadow." Jumping back into the car, they plug the address into the GPS and head for Tia's workplace.

Over an hour later, they pull into the parking lot for one of the most famous pyrotechnic companies in LA. Well known for its special effects and large-scale productions, FF Productions is housed in a large warehouse in an industrial area of LA.

Tatiana looks around. "Surely they don't make them here. It seems like too much of a risk with all these other buildings around."

Ruby's eyes follow the same path, and she shrugs. "It's probably just storage. It doesn't look fancy enough to be a display room, so I guess this is where all the planning happens."

They ring the doorbell set into the wall of the large concrete building and wait for someone to answer. A young girl, probably in her late teens, responds, looking a little confused to see people at the door.

"Can I help you?" she asks warily.

"Hi, we're looking for Tia Blackwood," Tatiana replies. "We were told she works here."

"Yeah, she does, but she's not here," the girl says and goes to shut the door, but Ruby sticks her foot in the way.

"Do you know when she will be back?" Ruby's voice holds a hint of steel and impatience.

The girl rolls her eyes. "They are all up at the Toronto International Fireworks Festival. They won't be back for a few weeks." Ruby moves her foot as she gapes at Tatiana in shock, and the girl manages to slam the door shut.

"Shit, she's practically on our back doorstep." Tatiana groans while Ruby's brain goes into planning mode.

She starts to head back toward the car with

Tatiana following. "Right, new plan now that we're zero for two."

They climb in and head back toward the airport.

"We'll go up to Eureka and grab Meadow, and then we'll head home and nab Tia on the way." Ruby nods her head in determination, and Tatiana just laughs.

"You're the boss." She leans back in her seat and observes Ruby's fiercely determined, but downright dangerous, driving all the way back to the airport.

Marijuana Ice~cream Recipe

Please be aware that Marijuana is illegal in Australia, so this recipe has not been tested, but it does appear to have good reviews from the website I got it from. It's all for a bit of fun. I would love to hear if anyone actually makes it.

- 2 to 2.5 grams of marijuana. Please be aware different marijuana strains cause different reactions. Maybe pick one that is not going to send you to sleep, unless that is what you are going for.
- 500 ml of cooking cream. The fat content is higher and thicker, which helps preserve all the properties of the marijuana.
- 2 tablespoons of butter.
- 75 grams of sugar. You can substitute a healthier alternative, like stevia, agave, maple, coconut, or birch syrup, but why would you?

- 2 ripe bananas. The riper, the better. They give better flavor and are easier to work with and prepare, and let's face it, no one actually likes to eat overripe bananas.
- A pinch of salt.
- A big old splash or 2 tablespoons of rum if we are getting technical.
- 5 tablespoons of honey. If the honey is pure, excellent, if not, who cares.

Gather your ingredients. Before we start, let's talk about decarboxylation.

When you smoke or vape cannabis, the process of decarboxylation is produced, in which the THCa of cannabis becomes THC. When this happens, you can enjoy the high that each different variety of marijuana offers.

But when it comes to cooking it, it's different.

First off, you need an oil or fat product, such as cream, in this case, so that it catches the properties of marijuana.

Secondly, you need to heat the marijuana buds to create the process of decarboxylation.

If you want your ice cream to cause a high, you will need to keep the marijuana buds in the oven—which you will have preheated for 10 minutes beforehand. That should do it.

Let's make ice cream.

Step 1: In a deep pot, heat the cream over a medium heat (so it doesn't burn) and stir slowly with a wooden spoon. Then add butter, salt, and sugar, stirring constantly.

Step 2: Once they are mixed, add the cannabis that you have broken up with the help of a grinder or, if you prefer, you can do it manually, although it will take longer.

S*tep 3:* Mush a banana in a clean bowl or plate with a fork. When ready, add it, along with the rum and honey, to the above mixture. Allow it to cool and then whisk everything together with a blender until creamy.

Step 4: Pour the mixture into a container that you can then put in the freezer. An ice cream container is probably the most practical to use. Place it in the freezer for at least four hours.

WARNING: Keep out of reach of children and those pesky teenagers. Oh, and probably really old people too.